From the time Soaring Hawk diagnoses his sister's illness as an infestation of angry fish-spirits, we enter another reality—the reality of the ancient world of the Cherokee Indians.

Young Soaring Hawk, an apprentice medicine man to his powerful uncle, Fighting Bear, is confident of his abilities, but Redbird's illness changes suddenly and conjury is suspected. Soaring Hawk blames Scratcher, Fighting Bear's arch rival. Drawn into a desperate battle for mystical power, the young medicine man knows that Redbird will die if his enemy prevails.

At Soaring Hawk's side as he conjures against Scratcher is Owl, a man of mysterious ways and awesome knowledge and power, and Chestnut Bread, Scratcher's "daughter." Her devotion to her friend Redbird, and her growing love for Soaring Hawk, leads her to defy the ways of her people. She is scorned by those around her, but stands firmly with Soaring Hawk and his family against the terror of evil forces.

JOYCE ROCKWOOD was born in Ames, Iowa, and spent most of her early years in Tifton, Georgia. She graduated Phi Beta Kappa from the University of Georgia with a degree in anthropology. Her husband is also an anthropologist; they live near Danielsville, Georgia. This is Ms. Rockwood's first novel.

THE LAUREL-LEAF LIBRARY brings together under a single imprint outstanding works of fiction and nonfiction particularly suitable for young adult readers both in and out of the classroom. The series is under the editorship of Charles F. Reasoner, Professor of Elementary Education, New York University.

LONG MAN'S SONG

Joyce Rockwood

Fic
Roc
AC

Published by
Dell Publishing Co., Inc.
1 Dag Hammarskjold Plaza
New York, New York 10017

Copyright © 1975 by Joyce R. Hudson

8/28/79 BJT 1.19

Laurel-Leaf Library ® TM 766734,
Dell Publishing Co., Inc.

ISBN: 0-440-94946-7

Reprinted by arrangement with Holt, Rinehart and
Winston.

Printed in the United States of America

First Laurel-Leaf printing—February 1978

Foreword

The North American Indian has provided stimulus for countless books, far out of proportion to the Indian's numerical significance in any roster of American ethnicity. Many historical reasons can be adduced to account for this popularity. In the traditional Western world view, Indians were regarded as savages or at best barbarians, a fixed lower rung on an assumed ladder leading upward, to civilization. In contrast, such other, less exotic ethnic folk as the Irish, Scotch, Jewish, Polish, Scandinavian, and Italian immigrants, and even involuntary immigrants like blacks, were seen as riders on a variable-speed escalator to respectable status in American society. The idea of Indians as creatures of history, or to use the more familiar stereotype, members of a "vanishing race," thus provided an ideal vehicle to contrast "us" to "them." Surely Indians could never be a sufficient threat to move into our neighborhoods. As a dying species separated from us by time and culture, the Indian could safely be endowed with an inherent native nobility, a pristine simplicity in his life-style. He could serve as a prototype for Natural Man or Ecological Man or Mystical Man. These images of the Indian, then, are our own continuous creations, serving our own conceptual ends; Indians become a projection by which we balance off our chronic ambivalence over the good and evil, content and discontent, and freedom and constraint generic to our own civilization.

Akin to this naïve, although pervasive, model of sociocultural development was a corresponding belief in a scale of mental evolution. Savages not only possessed a more rudimentary material culture and less complex forms of social organization, they were also less endowed intellectually. They were children of nature and, as such, thought like children. Or, as Shelley believed,

> *The Savage is to the ages,*
> *As the child is to years.*

Thus, given the logic (or illogic) of traditional Western thought, an affinity appears to exist between the Indian and the child.

On a psychological level as well, our culture has equated children and Indians. The imaginary Indian is seen as a free spirit, unaware of custom and convention, rebellious toward authority, impulsive and impetuous, following his own natural inclinations according to "Nature's simple plan." In the reputed *Sturm und Drang* of Euro-American late childhood and early adolescence, the Indian presumably serves as a figure with whom such young people can readily identify. Indian captivity, a recurrent nightmare for adults, was a wish fulfillment for their children.

We must be thankful to modern social science for having swept away most of these self-serving stereotypes and outmoded misconceptions. Indians are not "vanishing." The Indian population in the United States is growing rapidly. There are now about as many Indians as there were at the time of Columbus. Nor is the Indian culture "vanishing." Despite over two hundred years of "directed culture change," Indian people have for the most part maintained many of their institutions, as well as pride in their cultural heritage, while at the same time vying for the same standards of improved health care, housing, education, income, and civil rights as their "escalated" fellow Americans. Not only are Indians increasing numerically, but the social distance seems to be closing. Indians still vigorously defend their rights to reservation lands, but one of the more significant recent demographic trends is the Indian migration to cities. In addition, media advances have made mainstream America more accessible to all Americans. Indian children are reading children's books about Indians. It becomes vitally important, therefore, that books about Indians be faithful to their subject matter, that they avoid stereotypes and misconceptions, lest still more misinformation about Indians be disseminated and encoded into youthful minds. This book by Joyce Rockwood fulfills these criteria to a praiseworthy degree.

Long Man's Song is ethnologically accurate to a scholar's satisfaction. Even more severe critics, the Cherokees themselves, will, I think, approve of this book. The author has researched her subject and she displays a rare understanding of the underlying structure of traditional Cherokee society. Many writers of Indian books use a limited amount of research in constructing a story. All too frequently, ethnographic facts or presentations of real-life Indians are served up as extraneous asides or mere adornments rather than as integral elements in the plot. A patina of authenticity is achieved, but the story line remains essentially non-Indian.

This book is exceptional in that it is not only faithful to ethnographic data, it sets these facts into appropriate cultural contexts and articulates them admirably and with feeling. These are real Cherokees, not wooden stage props uttering foreign lines and performing alien roles in a cultural vacuum.

Yet these considerable virtues have not been achieved at the expense of literary worth. The plot of *Long Man's Song* is finely crafted. The descriptive passages are rich and resonant, the characters are real, their actions comprehensible. The vibrations and tensions of Cherokee life quickly reveal themselves. This is a finely written, accurately portrayed, morally responsible, and thoroughly enjoyable book about real

Indians. As such, it may be the first of its kind; I hope it's not the last.

Raymond D. Fogelson
Associate Professor, Department of Anthropology
University of Chicago

Acknowledgments

This book owes a great debt to my husband, Charles Hudson. As an anthropologist, he has shared his intellectual life with me to the fullest extent, and his unique understanding of the Indians of the southeastern United States has thereby become my own. Thanks are due also to Duane King, Laura H. King, Katherine G. Rockwood, and Raymond D. Fogelson for reading the book before publication and offering valuable suggestions.

To the Reader

This is the story of Soaring Hawk, a young Cherokee Indian living in the southern Appalachian Mountains in a time before the voyage of Columbus. Soaring Hawk is a fictitious character, but the Cherokee people are real, and in the pages of this book their ancient way of life has been portrayed as accurately as the record of history will allow.

The Cherokees were storytellers. Two of the stories they tell in this book, the story of Copper and the story of the man who married Thunder's sister, are adapted from Cherokee tales collected by James Mooney, an anthropologist who worked among the Cherokees of North Carolina in the nineteenth century.

J.R.

One

In a breechcloth and barefooted, with a short cape of turkey feathers about his shoulders, Soaring Hawk hurried along the path. Redbird, his sister, was sick. And he was on his way to get his uncle.

On either side of him, the corn stood tall and tasseled. Only yesterday Big Turtle had sent runners to the people up and down the river telling them that in fourteen days the corn would be ripe and it would be time for the celebration of the new year. It would be Soaring Hawk's seventeenth New Corn Festival, the seventeenth summer of his life.

Soaring Hawk tossed his head to feel the new bird skin he had just fastened in his hair. It was the feathered skin of a chickadee, the bird that knows things and always tells the truth, and Soaring Hawk was wearing it to remind people that he was an apprentice medicine man. Like the chickadee, he knew things and could speak truly. The new hairpiece made him feel different today—more handsome, more striking than before.

As he approached the square, he could see a group of his friends preparing for a game in the chunky yard. Several of the older men stood watching, their bets already on the ground. Although in a hurry, Soaring Hawk could not resist stopping for a moment. He pulled his cape about his shoulders against the chill of dawn.

"Someone doesn't have his throwing pole," Hard Mush said.

"Someone is not playing this morning," answered Soaring Hawk.

"What is it, brother? Are you afraid June Bug might beat you?" Everyone laughed. Soaring Hawk was one of the town's best chunky players and June Bug of late had been absolutely the worst.

"It is not fear you see—it's generosity," Soaring Hawk said with a grin. "Without me in the game, June Bug can have that good day he's been waiting for. I'd like to stay and watch him make fools of you all, but I have business with my uncle."

As he began walking away, Hard Mush and June Bug joined him. "If you could play chunky as well as you hunt, then maybe I could beat you," said June Bug, and he and Hard Mush began to laugh.

Soaring Hawk hardly winced. He was sensitive about the bad luck he had been having at hunting, but joking was a way of life with his people and he had learned long ago not to let it get the best of him. "What I really need," he said with a smile, "is for my family to learn to eat chunky stones."

"Then maybe you wouldn't be thinking so much about chestnut bread," said Hard Mush, and he and June Bug fell into such a fit of laughter that they could hardly continue walking.

Soaring Hawk groaned. He could not keep anything from his friends, not even his secret love for Chestnut Bread, his sister's closest friend.

"Chestnut bread?" he said. "Why should I think about that? If there is any food on my mind, it's corn—tender, juicy roasting ears just off the stalk. I can almost taste it now."

"But that can't be all you have on your mind," said June Bug, dropping the subject of Chestnut Bread and probing instead for what he and Hard Mush were really after. "A man always has more to think about than corn."

"That is true," said Soaring Hawk. "My sister is ill today."

The other two fell silent.

He added, "It looks like it's only some small thing that's causing it. I'll be helping with the cure today, but I expect to be back playing chunky by tomorrow."

Hard Mush and June Bug said they hoped that the thing that had gotten to Redbird was small, then turned back to the square. Soaring Hawk wished them well in the game, especially June Bug, then followed the path through the vegetable garden that led up to the homestead of Fighting Bear's wife. On one side of him stood old woman corn with vines of squashes and pumpkins rambling about her feet and beans and gourds hanging heavily on her stalks. On the other, great golden sunflower heads swayed gently in the early morning breeze.

But Soaring Hawk did not see the garden. He had no time to think about mother earth and her fruits. His one thought had to be of Redbird, and the possibility of being put in charge of her cure. Already in his apprenticeship he had been allowed to do some cures. But always the causes had been obvious and the cures simple. At times he had become very pleased with himself, feeling that he really knew things and that he was on his way to becoming as good and powerful a medicine man as his uncle. But at other times he wasn't sure. It sometimes seemed to him that anyone with a little knowledge could do these simple cures. He had especially begun to doubt himself in recent days. He had failed to change his hunting luck with the deer songs Fighting Bear had given him. What he needed was a real test of knowledge and power, one with results he could see. Redbird's illness, which seemed somewhat complicated but not very serious, might be just the thing. Yet much as he hoped his uncle would let him do the cure, he was uneasy at the prospect. Suppose he tried it and failed? He was not anxious to face that possibility, and whether he would today or not was going to be up to Fighting Bear, his mother's brother.

Fighting Bear was an important man in the town, second in white power and influence only to Big Turtle, the man who was chief in times that were white. White was the color of peace and happiness, of long life and sacred knowledge, and as long as the people were not at war, it was the beloved white men who led the councils. But when war came and times were red, the warriors with red power stepped to the front. Red was the color of success, of triumph over the enemy, and only the red war chief could lead the people to victory. When peace was restored, the town always became white again. Some of Soaring Hawk's friends were waiting for war, and for a chance to be great warriors. But Soaring Hawk was not. He intended to prove himself as a white medicine man, not as a red warrior.

As he drew near the central yard of the homestead, Soaring Hawk could smell food simmering in the large clay pot on the outside fire. His uncle was sitting on a cane mat beside the door of the summer house.

"Come have some breakfast, Nephew. Deer Foot has cooked some of the best venison stew you have ever tasted."

Soaring Hawk looked hungrily into the pot. "I know how good it would be, Uncle, but I'm keeping my stomach empty for curing this morning."

"Is that so? And just who has placed such confidence in your great wisdom and experience?"

Soaring Hawk grinned. "Nobody. But Redbird is sick, and Mother thinks you should come home and see about her before the thing gets too serious. I'm just hoping to be your assistant."

"Of course you will be that," said Fighting Bear, reaching for the walking stick that leaned against the wall of the summer house. He used the stick to pull himself to his feet. "You can tell me about the symptoms as we go."

They set out at once. As they left the yard Fighting Bear gave a backward glance at the stew pot. "I know that stew is good," he said. "I tasted it last night. I suppose it will be gone by the time I get back."

Soaring Hawk laughed. "Why not let me do all the cures? Then you wouldn't have to fast anymore."

"It must be that little chickadee that makes you so powerful," his uncle answered with a smile.

As they drew near the square, some of the men waved to Fighting Bear. "Come sit with us, Brother," called Big Turtle. "We have some things to decide to-day."

"Mother's waiting for us," whispered Soaring Hawk.

"I'll just give them a moment," said Fighting Bear, and he limped over to the arbor where the men were sitting.

The arbors in the square were long, open structures with rows of seats inside and leafy boughs laid over the roof frame to keep out the sun and rain. They were ar-ranged around an open danceground and served as a summer counterpart of the townhouse which stood nearby on a low, flat-topped, earthen mound. The townhouse was used mainly in winter. The square, with its arbors and danceground, its chunky yard and its townhouse, was the gathering place for the people of Raventown. During the day the older men came here to smoke and talk, to arrange things, and to watch the boys play their games of skill. But when the sun went down and it was too dark to hunt or work the crops or do the homestead chores, all sorts of people came to the square—men and women, young and old. They came to meet each other, some as friends, some as lov-ers; they came to catch up on the news and listen to stories; some came to sit at the councils and speak their minds; and many came just to be there, because to be in the square was to be in the center of things, to feel the heartbeat of the town.

While waiting for his uncle, Soaring Hawk joined a group of men who were watching the game in the chunky yard. These were red men, warriors.

"What's the betting?" he asked, nodding toward two

piles of goods on the ground. The larger pile contained a pair of moccasins, two rabbit skins, a pair of ear ornaments, a beaver skin, and four fine-looking arrows. In the smaller pile were only two things, a knife with a deer antler handle and a small beaded pouch.

"Most are saying Barking Dog will be the first to win four throws," said Bent Nose. "The small pile says it's going to be Hard Mush."

"How are they doing?"

"It's Barking Dog with three and Hard Mush with two. Do you want to throw something down?"

"Now?"

"Go ahead. The game's not over."

"I'll be leaving soon with my uncle. You wouldn't have a chance to win anything back."

"It could work the other way, couldn't it? Throw something down if you want."

Soaring Hawk glanced at the players at the end of the chunky yard. Hard Mush and Barking Dog stood side by side with their throwing poles. In one hand Barking Dog held the little stone chunky wheel. At any moment now he would send it rolling toward the other end of the yard, and as it sped along the smooth clay surface, the two of them would hurl their poles after it, each trying to make the red mark on his pole end up closer to the chunky stone when it finally rolled to a stop.

Turning back to the gamblers, Soaring Hawk took off a beaded bracelet and threw it onto the small pile. "I'll take Hard Mush!"

"I'll wear that bracelet home," laughed Bent Nose. Soaring Hawk laughed too.

A few moments later he rejoined his uncle with not only his bracelet but four new arrows in his hand and a rabbit skin on his belt.

Fighting Bear chuckled. "That chickadee works well for you," he said. But as they turned to leave the square, his face grew serious. "Tell me what is wrong with my niece," he said.

"I think it's only a small thing," Soaring Hawk began. "She has lost her appetite, mainly, and she's becoming blue. She seems to be losing more spirit every day."

"Just how many days has this thing been going on? Why wasn't I called earlier?"

"It started two days ago. At first it seemed like nothing. She took only a little from the food pot, but she said she was just tired. Then yesterday she ate no breakfast at all and took only a bite or two for supper. Mother had hoped you would come by last night. This morning Redbird still couldn't eat and she's getting weak. Mother fixed a bed for her by the fire in the summer house and sent me to bring you home."

Fighting Bear asked no more. As they walked along Soaring Hawk began to think about his last words. If they wanted Fighting Bear to be at home, they had to go and get him from where he lived, because home and where one lived were two different places for a married man. For a woman it was different. She always lived at home. When she married, her husband left his home and came to live in hers. It was always her home, never his. The children were hers. As long as her mother and her mother's sisters and her own sisters were alive, they would also live there with their own husbands and children. If a grown man wanted to return to his own home, he had to go back to the homestead of his sisters. They would always welcome him as one who belonged because they were his lineage, his own flesh and bone. There he would find his heirs, the children who would carry on his line. They were his sisters' children and, if he were an old man, the children of his sisters' daughters, and because they belonged to his lineage, they also belonged to him.

"Redbird should have at least two daughters," Soaring Hawk said.

Fighting Bear gave him a puzzled look.

Soaring Hawk shrugged. "I was thinking about things."

"It's true," said Fighting Bear. "We will need more daughters for our lineage if it's ever to grow. But you should not speak such thoughts aloud."

The rebuke was gentle, but it stung nonetheless, and Soaring Hawk walked in silence waiting for the explanation that in his heart he already knew.

"A terrible burden has fallen to your sister," said Fighting Bear. "You should try to help her feel it less, not more. My mother, your beloved grandmother, suffered greatly because she too was an only daughter and wanted so much to increase the lineage by giving it many daughters. All through her life, even until she died this last cold winter, she was always grieved that she was never able to give your mother and me another sister. The same agony that she had experienced she passed on to her own beloved daughter. And now, to your mother's sorrow, she herself has passed it on to yet another generation, to Redbird. My heart gets blue when I think about it."

"It is a sad lineage, isn't it," said Soaring Hawk. "With Grandmother gone to the Darkening Land there are only the four of us left—you and Mother, and Redbird and I. A lineage with only four people is so pitiful my friends don't even make jokes about it. If only somewhere along the way there had been more daughters. Then we would have a big, happy homestead, one full of people like all the others."

"Ours is happy enough," said Fighting Bear. "We should be thankful that each generation has always had a daughter that lived to bear another daughter. At least we are never robbed of hope."

"Sometimes," said Soaring Hawk, "I find myself wishing that when I get married the children born to my wife would belong to our people and not to hers."

"What foolishness. Of course they will be your wife's children. They'll belong to nobody's lineage but hers. Nothing can change the way the world is."

Soaring Hawk fell silent. They came at last to their homestead. His father was sitting in the yard carving a stone pipe that for weeks he had been working on in his spare time. Fighting Bear went directly into the summer house, while Soaring Hawk paused to talk to his father.

"You did not go hunting," he said, though he was not really surprised that Black Fox had changed his plans. People always made an effort not to seem worried when someone was sick, but until the illness was diagnosed, every heart remained uneasy.

"I know it's just some small thing that has gotten to your sister," said Black Fox, "but I'm curious to know what it is. I would probably wonder about it all day in the woods, and with my mind on too many things I doubt I would find so much as a rabbit. You probably know yourself how that is."

Soaring Hawk shrugged. He was not in a mood to discuss his hunting problem.

"Those are fine arrows you have there," said Black Fox.

Soaring Hawk smiled. "I bet on my friend Hard Mush. They all thought Barking Dog would beat him—he almost always does. But I've been watching Hard Mush's game lately. I thought this might be his day to start winning."

"Who lost his arrows?"

"Bent Nose. He lost that laugh of his, too."

Black Fox chuckled. "He'll find it again." He turned the carving over in his hand, studying it, deciding what part to work next.

Soaring Hawk said, "It's going to be a frog, isn't it? I can see it now."

Black Fox nodded.

"It will be a good pipe," said Soaring Hawk.

"Perhaps. But not so good as your uncle's bear pipe. Owl made that. Maybe when I am as old as Owl I'll be able to make a pipe that is as fine as that one."

"I think you will, Father."

Black Fox shook his head with a smile. "You'd better go in," he said. "You'll miss the cure."

Soaring Hawk left him and went into the summer house. A smoky haze hung in the room, gathering thick in the ceiling near the smoke hole. From the opening in the roof a shaft of light came down and fell upon the small fire in the hearth. The cane mat that hung in the doorway had been fastened back and the early morning sun streamed in, lighting the colorful mats that covered the walls. It was a two-room house, rectangular in shape. The walls were made of woven saplings plastered with mud, and the roof was thatch. Around the walls were bunks for sleeping and lounging, and on one of these, on layers of soft skins, Redbird lay listlessly. Across the room Easy Dancer, Soaring Hawk's mother, sat weaving one of her beautiful designs into a large pack basket. She seemed to feel easier now that her brother was home. Fighting Bear was sitting near Redbird, checking her over, asking about symptoms. He turned to Soaring Hawk when he came in.

"If you want to help me, Nephew, that will be all right. But I have been thinking that perhaps you should do the cure yourself. I have given you all the beloved words and knowledge I have and told you all the beloved stories I know to explain these things. If you are to be a medicine man who knows things, then you ought to be able to cure your sister. I think it is only a small thing that has gotten to her."

For a moment Soaring Hawk stood silent. This was what he had been waiting for. He was nervous, but he tried to hide it. "I know things, Uncle, because you have taught me well. I would like to do the cure."

Fighting Bear nodded and stepped back to the fire. Easy Dancer glanced briefly at her son and then turned back to her basket, seemingly unconcerned. That more than anything else made Soaring Hawk feel confident as he sat down beside Redbird.

There was not a great deal to be learned from the way Redbird looked or felt. The real answers in medicine were found in dreams and experiences, and it was

Soaring Hawk's task to find these out and interpret them. He had to be able to follow the right trail and ask the right questions. What warnings had been given? What rules broken? What enemies made? What forces in this vast world had been offended or put off-balance? The cure would never work unless the truth about things had been discovered.

For a time he sat quietly, collecting himself, considering the best way to begin. Then he began speaking to Redbird in a low voice. "It could be, Sister, that you feel like this because the spirit of a dead loved one is seeking your company on the long road to the Darkening Land, where the sun sets. The ghost acts in love, not malice, but it is not good for you if you are being beckoned this way. So that is why I want to know if our beloved grandmother has come into your thoughts or your dreams."

"No, I don't think it's that," Redbird said softly. "I've had only the briefest thoughts of her since we went to the river and washed ourselves free of her. I think we did that well enough to speed her on her way alone, and by now her journey is probably over. I don't think she's the one who is causing this."

Soaring Hawk had himself doubted that their grandmother was the cause. He too had felt that the river ceremony for her had been a good one; yet he had wanted to start with the most obvious possibility. "Let's think more about your dreams, then," he said. "Have you had any dreams about snakes lately?"

Redbird thought for a moment and then shook her head.

"Are you sure? Think hard."

"No, I would have remembered snakes."

"Well, how about fish? Have you had any fish dreams?"

Redbird thought even longer this time because fish dreams would be easier to forget. "No," she said finally. "None at all."

Soaring Hawk caught himself shifting uneasily. It

had been assumed that Redbird's saliva was spoiled. Spoiled saliva was what usually caused a loss of appetite and despondency. The question was, who had caused it? If it was their grandmother's ghost who had done it, or fish or snake spirits in a dream, then the sickness would be considered only a small thing.

But there were other, more serious causes of spoiled saliva. Someone in the village could have bad feelings for the family; someone who knew things could be using knowledge to work evil. This is what everyone had been silently hoping against because then it would be conjury, and conjury was no small thing. Conjury could even mean death.

"Think hard, Sister," Soaring Hawk implored. "Think back as far as you can. Did you never dream of fish? Not even once?"

Redbird thought for a long time. "No," she finally said. "Not once."

Two

Soaring Hawk was apprehensive. He would have liked to give the cure back to Fighting Bear, but that would have been the wrong thing to do. If he wanted to be more than just an apprentice medicine man he would have to go on with it himself. But how? He had never dealt with conjury before. What was he supposed to do? It seemed he had forgotten everything. He sat powerless and frightened, his face burning with shame. In his dreams he had always been stronger than this.

"I know!" said Redbird, sitting up suddenly in her bed. "I know what it is! I remember it now!"

Everyone turned to look at her.

"I remember a fish dream! A terrible dream! How could I have forgotten it? It was early in the spring when the weather had just begun to warm. One night after I had been fishing I had this dream. I don't remember everything about it, only that I had fallen into a giant basket of rotten fish. Somehow the fish were still alive, and they were squirming and flopping around all over me and blowing foul breath in my face. my   all I can remember, except that I was

Bear
nsult   tell us about it then?"
always
          They   get sick, I suppose. I decided it
          winter   n a bad dream and thought no
          was not
          ose back   le to remember it," said Soar-
                    erything. Did you forget to

"No, I did that. I remember. I thanked each one as I put it in my basket. I always do."

"Then maybe something else you did made them angry. Perhaps something you didn't know you were doing."

"Maybe I caught too many."

"They may have thought so. And to get revenge they came in that dream and spoiled your saliva. Now their spirits are inside you."

"I suppose they waited until now to make me sick so I would have to stay in bed during the festival."

"Don't worry about that. A small thing like this can be cured in four days. If I hurry, we can start today."

"That sounds good," she said. "I think missing the festival would ruin my whole year."

Soaring Hawk felt pleased with himself. He was sure his diagnosis was good. He looked at Fighting Bear, and his uncle nodded approval.

Easy Dancer laid aside her basket in relief. She got up and began moving about the room—stirring the coals in the hearth, putting water on to heat, setting by the door the empty jars to be filled at the river. Her husband, Black Fox, had watched the proceedings from the doorway. As he stepped inside, her eyes smiled at him in greeting.

"I knew it was only something small," said Black Fox. He turned to Fighting Bear. "You are teaching my son well, Brother-in-Law."

"He learns well."

"That is because he has a good teacher. I'm going out now. It's late to be starting, but it could be that daughter will want meat tonight."

As Black Fox left the homestead, Fighting and Soaring Hawk went out to the yard to c about the details of the cure. Medicine men sought privacy when discussing important things walked to the far side of the earth-covered house, and though the small, round structure high enough to shield them from the eyes of th at the summer house, it was a barrier of sorts and politeness would honor it. Fighting Bear leaned quietly on his cane and gazed peacefully at the nearby garden. After several minutes Soaring Hawk realized that his uncle was waiting for him to speak. As the curer in this case, Soaring Hawk had the first word. He paused for a moment, collecting his thoughts, then spoke carefully.

"I have already said what I believe to be the cause. If you do not disagree with that, then I shall tell you what I would do to cure her." He paused. "These things you have taught me. For medicine I would gather bark from four poplar trees and roots from four snakeroot plants. These should be boiled together to make the medicine, and it should be rubbed on her elbows and knees."

"Why there?"

"Because they are joints, and joints are where intruders are likely to enter." He paused again to allow objections. As none came, he went on. "Her face should also be rubbed because that is where they blew their breath. These places that get rubbed should be blown upon, and after that she should drink a little of the medicine. It will all be done four times, from sunrise until noon, and it will be repeated for four days. She will have to fast during these morning treatments. As her curer I will have to do the same."

"What about your medicine bundle? What color will it be?"

"Red. They will have to give me a red skin for the bundle. It is the color of success over enemies and the color of the Sun Land. I think it would be especially good against the coolness of the fish spirits."

"You have spoken well," said Fighting Bear. "If you want to give the medicine four times before noon, you will have to hurry. Go now and get the skin from your mother and be on your way."

As Soaring Hawk turned to go, Fighting Bear settled himself down in a sunny spot beside the winter house.

"Aren't you coming back to the house?" asked Soaring Hawk.

"Not just now, Nephew. I think I'll sit here in the sun for a while and watch the corn get ripe."

The sun was not yet high in the morning sky as Soaring Hawk made his way toward the river. To avoid the public paths, he skirted around the outlying homesteads and cut through the middle of the town fields that filled the bottom lands along the river's course. Unlike the small family gardens near each house, these large fields were planted, cultivated, and harvested by all the men, women, and children of the town working together. In only a few days the town crier would be calling them to these fields to harvest the first of the new corn crop. At daybreak his call would carry from the top of the townhouse mound to the farthest corners of the village, and there would be excitement in the air as people descended on the fields with their corn baskets. All would be anxious to taste the first fresh morsels of new corn, but they would have to wait a little longer. When the new year was officially begun, there would be feasting, and they could have all the freshly roasted ears they could eat.

As Soaring Hawk made his way through the field, a little smile crept over his face at the thought of his uncle sitting back at the winter house watching the corn in the garden. He said he could *see* it get ripe. Soaring Hawk was inclined to believe him, even though he had probably been joking. He would believe almost anything his uncle said, for there were few medicine men anywhere who knew more about things than Fighting Bear did. Everyone knew this, and Fighting Bear was regarded with great respect by all. Easy Dancer often said that because of Fighting Bear's power the Deer people stood a little higher in the town.

Soaring Hawk was a Deer person because his lineage belonged to the clan that was called Deer. All of the people in all of the towns were divided into seven clans, and the size of each clan varied from town to town. Here in Raventown the Wolf clan was the strongest because it had five lineages, and some of those lineages were quite large even by themselves. The weakest clan in Raventown was the Deer clan with its single lineage. Having only one lineage in a clan was not itself so bad. Soaring Hawk's father's clan, the Bird people, also had just one lineage, but it was a lineage of normal size; it had almost thirty people in it. So here it was again—every problem always seemed to come back to rest on the tiny size of Soaring Hawk's lineage.

Even the problem with Scratcher was linked to it in a way. It was likely that if Fighting Bear had more clansmen to back him up, Scratcher would not be so openly against him. Scratcher belonged to the Wolf clan, and he was one of the more powerful and ambitious men in Raventown. He was highly regarded as the town's best curer of arthritis, and his name came from that part of the curing ceremony where the aching joints are scratched with briars before the medicine is rubbed on. But Scratcher's ambitions could not be satisfied and he was always seeking more power. He had been working his way up among the medicine men, and everyone knew that he now had his eye on Fighting Bear's position as the head medicine man. It was because of this that the rivalry had developed between the two men.

Soaring Hawk remembered well what had happened last summer. There had been almost more rain than the crops could stand and Scratcher had spoken out loudly against Fighting Bear. It had all started in the spring when the land had become so dry that the little seedlings nearly died from thirst. Fighting Bear had had no choice but to hold a rain ceremony, and rain it did, in torrents. Then Scratcher accused him of having been a fool. "In spring the rains always come sooner or later," Scratcher had said, and he told the people that the rain ceremony had only served to bring on too much rain. Scratcher was such a good speaker that people began to listen to him, until finally Fighting Bear had to hold a public ceremony to stop both the rain and the talk. It was a difficult ceremony to perform, yet Fighting Bear showed his power and skill by causing the rains to diminish just enough to save the crops and yet not so much as to bring back the drought.

"Scratcher was wrong," people said then. Soaring Hawk had seen the ugly expression on Scratcher's face when they teased him about it. "It may be true that there is a foolish man among us," someone would say, "but Fighting Bear is not the one." Then everyone would laugh and look at Scratcher. Ever since this defeat, Scratcher's heart had been red toward Fighting Bear. It was red with desire for victory just as a warrior's heart is red, but in this battle the weapon of each man was power—the power that comes from knowing things.

Soaring Hawk's thoughts ended abruptly as the cornfield through which he had been walking. The little river glimmered before him in the morning sun. It was not a wide river and not deep, for here in the mountains few rivers were large. In most places he could wade across it without getting his breechcloth wet, although in some spots, often in the bends, there were deeper pools where the children played on hot summer afternoons.

To Soaring Hawk's people every river and stream was a part of Long Man, who had his head in the mountains and his feet in the sea. They believed that Long Man was a keeper of great power. When people wanted to ask things of the forces that guide the world, they would go to water at daybreak and stand looking upstream toward the rising sun. As a medicine man said the beloved words for them, and as they immersed themselves in the flowing waters, answers would be given to them and their lives would be strengthened. Long Man had the power to do these things. Those who knew things could listen to Long Man and hear what he was saying. Soaring Hawk himself had spent many quiet times listening to the waters. Even though what he heard made him feel things in his heart, he could not always turn these feelings into words. He was grateful for the feelings, but he knew that a man or woman who really knew things would be able to hear more.

It was because Soaring Hawk knew that the river had so much to give him that he came here now to look for medicine. Plants that grew within the sound of the river would be more powerful than those that had never had a chance to listen to the waters. No one had ever told him this, but he knew nonetheless that it was true. Not all medicines could be found near rivers, but many could, including the poplar tree and snakeroot plant that he needed today. Already he knew where four poplar trees grew, and he knew of two places where he had seen snakeroot. But he would have to find a third and then a fourth snakeroot plant before he could gather the medicine. It was always necessary to locate all the medicines that were needed before gathering them. Then the last to be found was the first to be gathered, and so on back along the way until all of the medicines were wrapped in the bundle.

Soaring Hawk moved quickly along the riverbank, his eyes scanning both sides of the path, and it was not long before he found the two more snakeroot plants he needed. At the last of these he stopped and brought out the red deer skin that was tucked in his belt. He spread the skin neatly on the ground, and using a sharp digging stick, he found a root that grew eastward, toward the Sun Land. He used his flint knife to cut off a long piece of it, and he placed the root on the skin. Then he dropped a white shell bead into the ground where the root had been before. As he patted the dirt back in place, he thanked the snakeroot plant, saying that he hoped the white bead would compensate for the wonderful and powerful root that necessity had forced him to take away for medicine. Then, wrapping the root in the skin bundle, he waded across the river to take some bark from a poplar tree. He cut a small piece from the eastern, Sun Land side and added it to his medicine bundle; then he wedged a tiny shell bead into the bark near the tree's wound and whispered words of thanksgiving and praise.

He hurried along gathering the rest of the medicines, retracing his earlier steps and stopping at each tree or plant until at last he had only one more poplar tree to go. Just as he was about to cut this last piece of bark, a sound from the path ahead sent him slipping quickly and quietly into the cover of a thicket of mountain laurel. He listened and heard the very faint padding of bare feet upon the hard trail.

He was almost certain it was someone from the village, yet he stayed out of sight, remembering the many warnings Fighting Bear had given him about a medicine man's need for secrecy. Crouching in silence, he watched the path through the thick foliage of the laurel. Suddenly a tall man came into sight—it was Scratcher! He was carrying a bundle. Was it a medicine bundle? Soaring Hawk strained to get a better look, but Scratcher was already disappearing down the path.

If Scratcher was out gathering medicine, it meant that someone else in Raventown was sick. It was curious that Soaring Hawk had heard nothing about it at the square that morning. He tried to shrug it off as nothing important, but as he worked his way out of the thicket, a kind of uneasiness took root in his heart.

Quickly he went to the poplar tree to cut the last piece of bark. Before he left the river he tossed his medicine bundle into the water. It floated, as he knew it would, for he was sure he had done everything right. Satisfied that his medicine was powerful, he fished it out of the water and ran all the way home.

He stopped in the yard to show the bundle to Fighting Bear, and then he went inside, where Easy Dancer already had a small pot of water boiling on the fire. He handed her the bundle and watched as she dropped the pieces of root and bark into the pot. "It will have to boil down," he said. He turned to Redbird. "We'll probably have to go straight through in giving the medicine—no rests in between. Would you rather wait and start tomorrow?"

"No, I don't want to take an extra day unless we have to. I have too many things to do before the festival."

"I feel that way, too," said Soaring Hawk, and he sat down to wait and to review in his mind the words he would say with the medicine. The formula he had chosen was a simple one. He was going to call only on the Red Kingfisher who lived in the Sun Land of the Upper World. If the disease were more serious, he would use a formula that called on powers from all directions of the Upper World, which here would mean the Blue, Black, and White Kingfishers too. But for this illness he did not really think it would be necessary to go beyond the Red Kingfisher.

When the medicine was ready, he went to a basket under one of the bunks and brought out his gourd rattle and his gourd medicine dipper. He gave the dipper to his mother to be filled. Then Redbird was moved to a seat facing east, toward the open doorway and the Sun Land, and Soaring Hawk took his place standing before her. As the song of his rattle filled the air, Fighting Bear came and stood inside the doorway. Then Soaring Hawk began to chant the medicine formula, saying the words so quickly and so softly that no one could hear exactly what they were. No one, that is, except the Red Kingfisher—he could hear the words quite clearly as they were carried to the Upper World by the song of the gourd.

"Now then! Ha, you Red Kingfisher,
powerful force.
You live on high in the Sun Land.
Now you have been made to come down, it seems.
Your path has led you here,
And you are moving about in the treetops.

"The fish that have come to her are only ghosts,
   it seems.
They are only minnows, nothing more.
They thought they would not be found out.
Now they have been made slow and easy to catch.

"Now then! You have come near to listen,
   O Red Kingfisher.
Now you have come to take them away.
They are the very things you eat.
As you fly by they will be taken away from her.
Relief will be with her at once."

Soaring Hawk nodded to his mother, and Easy
Dancer rubbed medicine first on Redbird's right elbow,
and then on her left knee, then on her left elbow, and
finally on her right knee. The medicine formed a cross,
and crosses were powerful because they showed the
four directions of the world.

Soaring Hawk repeated the words to the Red Kingfisher, and then Easy Dancer blew her breath four
times upon each place where she had rubbed medicine.
Soaring Hawk sang the words a third time, and Easy
Dancer rubbed medicine first on Redbird's forehead,
then on her chin, then on her right cheekbone, and finally on her left cheekbone. Soaring Hawk sang the
words for the fourth time and Easy Dancer blew her
breath four times upon each of these places. Easy
Dancer then gave Redbird a little of the medicine to
drink. With this, the first giving of the medicine was
over.

Soaring Hawk stepped over to the door and looked
up at the sky. "It's nearly noon," he said. "We'll have
to go right on if we're to give it all four times."

"That's all right," said Redbird. "I don't need to
rest. I just want to get it over with."

Soaring Hawk came back and stood before her, and
the gourd once again began its song.

Three

At noon, when the curing was over, Redbird was offered a small dish of cold corn gruel. She accepted it willingly, for already her appetite was returning. Soaring Hawk watched her until his pride in what he had accomplished became so great that he was afraid the others would see it. Taking up his bow and quiver, he ducked outside into the bright sunlight. He was halfway across the yard before he stopped with a little grunt of annoyance. His new arrows. He had forgotten them. He would be teased for going back, but he wanted those particular arrows. Because he had won them, they might make a difference in the hunt.

Easy Dancer chuckled when she saw him. "Back already? What did you bring us?"

"I hope it's nothing bigger than a bear," said Redbird, and she laughed for the first time that day.

"I don't know if I should try to change my hunting luck or not," grinned Soaring Hawk as he picked up the four arrows and started out again. "What would people laugh at then?"

"Your good looks!" Redbird called after him.

Leaving the homestead behind, Soaring Hawk turned onto the path that ran northeast along the edge of the town toward the wooded mountains that rose abruptly at the valley's edge. He hesitated, remembering that the path passed by the homestead where Scratcher lived with his wives and their lineage. But then he laughed at himself, wondering why he should suddenly have become so nervous, and he continued on his way.

Through the lush vegetation of the river valley the path wound its way, a narrow aisle where no grass would grow. Smooth and hard from the countless bare and moccasined feet that had traveled over it for as long as the oldest memory, the path was as familiar to Soaring Hawk as his mother's face, and like his mother's face he sometimes loved it and sometimes did not notice it at all. Today he did not watch the homesteads going by, nor glance over at the shady groves, nor at the gardens, nor at the fallow fields basking lazily in summer's midday sun. He was preoccupied with his own thoughts, with the idea that he, Soaring Hawk of the Deer people, was now a real medicine man. So it was that on rounding one of the bends it was more reflex than anything else that whipped an arrow into his bow and sent it flying through a rabbit that had raised up to look at him.

"Not exactly what I had in mind," he muttered as he walked up to claim the kill. He used some grass to wipe the blood from the arrow before putting it back in his quiver. "Why couldn't you be a deer?" he said as he tied the dead animal to his belt. "But let your spirit go along. I give you my thanks—and my promise not to waste you."

Once again his feet padded silently along the path. The homestead of Scratcher's wives came in view, its many houses scattered beneath the shade of oak and hickory. Soaring Hawk remembered the morning's encounter at the river and he wondered again if Scratcher was curing someone today. He would probably find out later who it was—Fighting Bear would hear about it at the square.

"Hello there! Where's your sister?"

Soaring Hawk spun around to find Chestnut Bread smiling at him. She looked beautiful—barefoot, a skirt of soft deer skin hanging from her waist to her knees, her black hair tied in a knot behind her neck. He was glad to see her, but embarrassed that she had been able to come upon him unnoticed. He should have known to look for her here: Scratcher was her father's brother, the same as a father to her, and she often visited his wives' homestead. She was a daughter of their clan, for Scratcher and his brothers, who were Wolf people, had married women of the Paint clan. Their children, including Chestnut Bread, were Paint people.

Soaring Hawk gave her a little smile. "My sister is home today," he said. "Some little thing has gotten to her. She'll have to stay in for a few days, but if you went by, I know they would let you see her."

"This isn't a very good time to be sick. I hope it's something small."

"That's all it is. She's already feeling better. No one is worried."

"That's good," said Chestnut Bread. She looked silently at the ground. Soaring Hawk gazed off at the mountains and tried desperately to think of something else to say, anything to keep her from leaving. He remembered Scratcher.

"Is your father curing today?" He still looked at the mountains as he spoke. Chestnut Bread would know which of her fathers he meant because Scratcher was the only medicine man among them.

"No, I don't think he is," she said. "No one has come for him since I've been here."

"Oh. Well, he usually is out curing. That's why I asked. I was wondering who might be sick today. Who besides Redbird." His gaze left the mountains and wandered over to the homestead and stopped on the tall man rising to his feet in the yard. It was Scratcher. He took a few steps in their direction and stood staring at them. He seemed displeased, but he was too far away for Soaring Hawk to be sure.

Chestnut Bread saw him too. "I think my tall father wants me to come in," she said quietly, and she started at once toward the homestead.

"Wait!" said Soaring Hawk.

Chestnut Bread stopped.

He held out the rabbit he had killed. "Could you use fresh meat? I know it's not much, but I'd like you to take it if you think your clan mothers could use it."

Chestnut Bread smiled at him. "You are very generous. I'll take if if you want me to. It's always good to have more meat."

Soaring Hawk glanced over at the yard and was glad to see that Scratcher had sat down and turned his back to them. "You had better not tell him where you got it," he warned.

She nodded. "I wish they would end this feud. It's bad enough to have my tall father and your uncle always at each other, but now it's spreading through both the clans until it's Wolf people against Deer people. And me, even though I'm Paint, I have to respect my fathers. My tall father doesn't like for me to see Redbird anymore, but my own father, my gentle father, he thinks the feud should not go so far. He stands up for me against his brother on that. I wish there could be an end to all of it. My heart gets blue."

"Mine too," said Soaring Hawk. "But what about the rabbit?"

"I'll tell him I got it from a snare trap. There won't be any trouble. My clan mothers don't care about the feud."

"All right. If you think that will work. But you don't see many snared rabbits with holes in them."

Chestnut Bread looked down at the rabbit and laughed. "No, you don't, do you. But it doesn't matter. He won't be paying attention. Goodbye now. I've got to hurry."

As Soaring Hawk watched her go, his heart began to reel with joy. He could hardly believe what had just happened. He offered her game and she *took* it! She wanted him! Would she offer something back? If she did that, he would know for sure. He was so excited, he wanted to do something, jump around and yell, but not on a public path. So he ran, his feet beating swiftly over the hard trail, running as fast as he could go—away from the town, through the last of the outlying gardens, up into the mountains and the familiar solitude of the forest. There he stopped and closed his eyes, breathing deeply, savoring his happiness. He seemed to feel himself melt into the vibrant shadows, his heart uniting with the heart of the forest, the wind and the songs of the birds passing freely through him as if he were part of them.

He opened his eyes and the world returned. At first he stood grinning. Then he began to whoop and yell and leap around as he might have done in the most exciting of dances in the town square. But at last he stopped and tried to get hold of himself. Hunting was a serious business. It was what he had come for and it was time to get on with it. Yet he could not resist one last indulgence: "I've done so well today," he boasted aloud to the sky and the trees, "I've done so well that now I am going to bring home a deer! Just wait and see! A big fat buck!"

It was nearly sundown when Soaring Hawk came into the yard of his homestead. He gave three rabbits to his mother and sat down next to Black Fox. "What you have always said about boasting is true," he said. "It turns the forces of the world against you."

Black Fox chuckled.

Soaring Hawk said, "If I hadn't been proud and boastful today, I think I might have finally had good hunting again."

"You'll have another day," said Black Fox. "This won't go on forever. You know, sometimes it helps a person to settle down a little. Sometimes it is hard for a person to do well at some things if he always has too many other things in his mind."

"I think you are right, Father. I know you are." Soaring Hawk sat for a long time staring into the fire. Then suddenly he jumped to his feet. He had just made a decision. "Do you know where my uncle is?" he asked.

Black Fox nodded toward the summer house. "In there with your sister."

But just then Fighting Bear appeared outside. "Well now, here's my nephew the curer. He's back. From where? From hunting?"

"In a manner of speaking," grinned Soaring Hawk. "I was just coming to find you. Would you like to go out with me to look at the corn?"

Fighting Bear nodded, and the two of them walked together across the yard until they came to the same spot where they had consulted earlier. "Now, just what shall we talk about while we look at the garden again?" asked Fighting Bear.

"I guess it does look about the same," said Soaring Hawk. "But I wanted to talk to you."

"I wouldn't say it looks exactly the same," said Fighting Bear, "but that doesn't really matter, does it?"

Soaring Hawk shrugged, not sure if it did or not. He paused for a few moments to collect himself, and then he said, "I think we should take measures to protect the house against night-goers while Redbird is sick."

Fighting Bear suddenly became very serious. "Do you think that is necessary, Nephew? Your sister has only a small thing, you know. Nothing more than fish spirits. It is hardly a condition that would make her prey to night-goers. There are very many people in these parts who are in a worse condition than she is. They'll keep the night-goers busy. It is the ones who are too weak to resist that they're after. The old people and infants. The women in childbirth. They are the ones the night-goers want when they change into owls, or ravens, or balls of purple fire and fly through the night to terrorize us. So why worry about a strong young woman who is already recovering from a thing that was not very serious to begin with?"

Soaring Hawk was taken aback. He had not expected to have to argue his point, and now he realized that he did not really have good reasons to offer. "It's only a feeling I have," he said. "I feel she's not safe. That's all I can tell you."

It was Scratcher that worried him. He had seen him with a medicine bundle by the river. Yet, according to Chestnut Bread, Scratcher had not been called to cure anyone. A person gathering medicine for something other than curing might possibly be conjuring, doing people harm. Soaring Hawk was not ready to accuse Scratcher of evil conjury. It was too grave a charge even to mention unless he had more evidence.

But he knew the Deer people had to stay on their guard. If conjury were to make Redbird weaker during the night, there might be lurking outside in the darkness a night-goer who would make himself invisible and come into the house to steal her soul by taking out her liver or her heart. Then when daylight came, the night-goer would change back into a seemingly harmless man or woman living nearby, maybe even in Raventown itself, and poor Redbird would awake without even knowing that anything had happened. But she would become weaker and weaker, and in seven days she would waste away and die, and the years she was robbed of would be added to the life of the hateful night-goer who had attacked her.

Soaring Hawk could not bear to think of it. "We must do it, Uncle! My heart tells me this!" He stood tall, his eyes dark and flashing, his jaw set hard. He would not relent.

"A medicine man must always listen to his heart," Fighting Bear said quietly. "If your heart tells you this, then we will do what you say. There is no other choice."

For a moment Soaring Hawk stood silent, his face drawn. He had been ready for a confrontation, but already it had come and gone. The energy that had rushed into him began to drain away. "We'll have to hurry," he said dryly. "It's almost dark. I'll go back and get a black skin and make everything ready." He

turned and hurried back to the yard, leaving Fighting
Bear to hobble in at his own speed.

As he moved through the preparations, Soaring
Hawk felt a strangeness in himself. Something had
changed in him. He had spoken out back there not as
the apprentice, but as a medicine man. He put down
the tobacco pipe he was filling and looked out over the
valley. Even the land did not seem the same. Suddenly
Soaring Hawk felt very old—as old as the mountains
that stood over the valley watching the generations of
his people come and go, as old as Long Man River and
Ancient Fire.

The ceremony against night-goers was carried out
smoothly. Afterward there was a sumptuous meal of
venison from a deer Black Fox had brought in, and everyone was glad to see Redbird eat some of the meat.
Night had fallen, and it was that good time of the evening when kinsmen and friends relaxed together
around their outside fires. Redbird was not allowed to
come out, though, and Black Fox stayed in the summer
house to keep her company. Outside, Fighting Bear
and Easy Dancer sat quietly by the fire and watched
the flames dancing about. Soaring Hawk was there too,
stretched out on his back as he looked up at the stars
and listened to the songs of the night. Loudest was the
song in his own heart:

> The world is white and peaceful.
> There is nothing to fear.
> With our tobacco smoke we have put a great
>   black Serpent spirit around our house.
> No night-goer can escape his watchful eye.
> We are following the beloved path.
> Our path is white.
> Our path is peaceful.

The other songs were the same ones he always heard
on a summer night. The song of laughter drifted over

the town as jokes and stories flew like moths around the fires. Beyond the town the whippoorwills sang, and in the river bottom the frogs blended their voices with crickets and katydids.

The moon had not risen, and the darkness of the night reminded Soaring Hawk of one of his favorite stories. "Tell us about that dark night on the mountain, Uncle. It's been a long time since we've heard that story."

"You've heard it so many times you could tell it yourself," laughed Fighting Bear.

"No, I couldn't. Not like you do. It didn't happen to me."

Fighting Bear straightened. He concentrated on refilling his pipe, then gazed off into the darkness of the night. After a long silence he began to speak. "It happened in the fall of the year. I was a young man, not much older than Soaring Hawk is now. One day I left the village with two of my companions, Big Turtle and Jumper. We were going up into the mountains to hunt bear. I had two good legs then, and I was considered a good hunter. In those days I was called Straight Shooter."

Fighting Bear paused to light his pipe.

Redbird called to them from the summer house. "It would be a nice thing if some people who were telling good stories would speak louder so that some people who have to stay inside can hear. That's all I have to say."

They all laughed, and Fighting Bear continued in a louder voice. "Some men in the town had told us they had seen good bear signs up in the mountain gap that we call Frog Place. But after we reached there, bad luck fell upon us so that after two days we still had not found a fresh trail. We decided that to cover more ground we would have to separate and go off in different directions. We agreed to return the next day to the place where we then stood, and off each of us went with high hopes of being the first to find a bear trail.

"It was late afternoon when I came to a little glade on the mountainside, and I knew right away that I had found what we were looking for. All the signs said that a bear had been there no longer than a day ago. I followed its trail a little way, but the sun was sinking and I decided to go back to the glade to make camp. I would go back for the others the next day, and we could easily pick up the fresh trail.

"I made a fire and ate some parched corn. Then I stretched out for a good night's rest. Just before I fell asleep I remarked to myself that the moon would be setting early.

"The next thing I knew I was awake and listening to the sound of a big animal crashing through the underbrush very close to me. I knew at once it was a bear. Nothing else would make so much noise. I bolted straight up and reached for my bow, but I was surrounded by darkness. The moon had set and my fire was out. Even the stars were covered with clouds.

"I tried to calm myself. Bears don't attack people unless they have to, I told myself. It was then that the idea came to me to simply move quietly out of its way. And that is what I thought I was doing when all of a sudden from right beside me there came a hideous growl! Then all I knew was fur and claws and pain and darkness, and the horrible foul odor of its breath. I remember thinking that this was what it was like to be killed. Then I remembered my knife. The very thought of it gave me new strength. I grappled like a madman until I managed to pull it from my belt. Using all the strength I had left, I struck out blindly at the place I thought the throat to be. With a terrible cry the bear sank to the ground. It was dead—and I was nearly dead too. I knew my leg was torn to pieces and I twisted my belt tightly around it, hoping that somehow I wouldn't bleed to death. I knew nothing after that.

"The next day my friends found me in that place. I was lying in a heap beside my tormentor. They used the bear's own skin to carry me home. For days I hung between life and death, but my medicine man was Owl, and his power was as great then as it is today. It was his power and knowledge that brought life back to me. But even Owl could not restore my leg. I was never again the fine hunter I had been. I never played another game of ball; never ran another race, never fought the battles I had trained for. And so I became a medicine man, and if you think about it, I think you can understand that I am not really very sorry for that dark night of terror on the mountain."

Fighting Bear sat back puffing gently on his pipe, gazing serenely into the fire. It was a long time before anyone broke the silence. "And since that night they've called you Fighting Bear," Easy Dancer added softly.

"Yes, and now Fighting Bear had better get back to his wife before she forgets what he looks like."

They all chuckled as they rose to their feet, and Black Fox came outside.

"Don't hurry off," he urged. "Stay the night."

"There is no reason for me to stay," smiled Fighting Bear. "There is a competent medicine man in charge here. I'll come back in the morning to see how the cure is coming along."

As Fighting Bear hobbled off into the night, Soaring Hawk went into the summer house and found Redbird already asleep. "Have a white sleep, Sister," he whispered softly. The low fire in the hearth shed only a dim light, and he had to search around before he found a blanket for himself. Going back outside, he wrapped himself in it and lay down once more by the fire, this time to drift to sleep with thoughts of Chestnut Bread. Easy Dancer and Black Fox sat up a while longer, talking together in low voices, but they too soon called it a day. Black Fox rolled up in a blanket across the fire from Soaring Hawk, and Easy Dancer went in to sleep near her daughter.

Soaring Hawk slept fitfully that night, tossing and turning until finally he found himself awake. He lay quietly, listening to the night, feeling that something out there had wakened him. Then he heard it, and a cold chill gripped his heart. From a nearby grove of trees came the eerie cry of a long-eared owl, the kind of owl that was called the night-goer owl because it was a favorite disguise of night-goers.

This is only an owl, Soaring Hawk told himself. It's no more than that. It will go away.

Then the call came again, closer than before. Soaring Hawk's heart began to pound. I know it's only an owl, he told himself again. There is no reason for a night-goer to come here. No one here is very sick. The house is protected. This is only an owl, and it will go away now.

He raised up on one elbow. If it came any closer, he was going to yell for the family. He didn't care if he woke the whole town.

For a long time he waited. At last the call came again, but now it was far away. With a sigh of relief he settled back into his blanket. I think it really was just an owl, he thought as he began drifting back to sleep.

Four

It was the afternoon of the third day of curing, and Redbird was feeling as well as she had ever felt. But feeling well did not mean leaving the summer house. Three days of curing were not enough. There had to be four. So Soaring Hawk was staying at the homestead doing some of the chores that his sister was unable to do, chores which neither June Bug nor Hard Mush would ever have to do. Their mothers had not only sisters to help them when a daughter got sick, but also other daughters, and even other women in their clans who were the same as sisters and daughters to them. June Bug's mother or Hard Mush's mother would never have to be home alone at times like this, doing all the work in the homestead. No one's mother but Soaring Hawk's.

Yesterday he had dressed a hide for her, the one from the deer his father had brought home that first day of the cure. And today he had filled the water jars at the river and wandered through outlying groves of trees gathering wood for the fire. When he finished those things, he had even pounded up some corn, some of the last in the granary.

Pounding corn was not something Soaring Hawk did well. The stubborn kernels in the hollow of the upright log seemed to move out of the way as he jabbed at them with the tall pounding stick. His mother and sister always worked a nice rhythm into their pounding. Soaring Hawk tried it, but only briefly, then let it go, afraid someone in the house would hear his lame ef-

forts and laugh. He was afraid, too, that someone passing by would see him pounding corn, and then the
word would get around that he was doing women's
work, and it would be a long time before the teasing
stopped. They might even start calling him Corn
Pounder. As he worked, his eyes and ears were on the
path. If he heard voices or laughter or saw a head bob-
bing along above the garden corn, he dropped the
pounding stick and tried to look busy doing something
else.

It took a long time to make cornmeal that way, but
when at last he finished, there was little else for him to
do, and he began to think of going to the square. He
had not been back to the square since he had won the
four arrows in the betting. That was the day he first
wore the chickadee in his hair, the day he began his
first big cure. He felt in his heart that he was different
now from the person he had been that morning. Today
he was close to being a real medicine man who thought
for himself instead of an apprentice who only followed
instructions. He was moving alone now, making his
own trail among the forces of the world, and they, the
forces of the world, were looking toward that trail—
were waiting for him, listening, watching.

Yes, this was a new day. Now there was more to
him. He thought for a moment. . . . It was the river
now. The river's day was dawning on his life, the
power of the river.

It seemed to Soaring Hawk that Long Man had always been calling him, inviting him to walk along his
banks or sit quietly watching the beauty of his rushing
waters and listening to his song. It must have been
Long Man himself who told Soaring Hawk always to
gather medicine from within the sound of the water so
that the herbs would be strong with the power and wisdom of the river. There was truth in that—Redbird
was already well.

Soaring Hawk could see that the trail he was making
for himself was a trail of water, a clear stream rippling

over a bed of smooth pebbles, winding secretly beneath
green boughs; a beautiful little river flowing down
through the mountains, down from the peaks, down
from the universe beyond. He shivered at the thought
of it. He had changed so much. Would they even know
him at the square?

He laughed at himself. They would not see a single
thing different about him. He would have to show
them. There would have to be something about him
that would tell them. But what could he wear that
would speak of the river? Not a fish skin in his hair—
he smiled to himself—not an eel around his neck; not
a live rattlesnake for a bracelet like the ones the Thunder Boys wore. Not a necklace made of river rocks,
nor a frog skin tobacco pouch, nor a string of tor-
toiseshell rattles on his leg like the ones women wore
to dances. Ridiculous things were coming to his mind.
A whirlpool for an arrow quiver. A waterfall for a
summer cape. A beaver for a hand ax. An otter for a
breechcloth.

Otter! That was it. He had an otter skin stored away
in the winter house, just waiting to be used. This otter
was more than an otter. There was something very
special about it. When he had killed it last winter, he
had intended to cut the tanned hide into strips for
thongs. But he had not done that. Because of the way
the animal had looked at him—*after* it was dead.

It had been very strange. A clean kill—one arrow
through the head. But suddenly, Soaring Hawk was
sorry. He wished that he could take back the shot and
let the otter swim away. He said prayers to the otter's
spirit, but still he felt badly. So he burned some cedar
incense, a gift to the spirits of all forest and water
dwellers. It had made no difference. Sorrow covered
his heart and nothing he could do helped to lift it
away. And when he picked up the otter, limp and ut-
terly lifeless, blood oozing out around the arrow shaft
and soaking into its dark brown fur, tears sprang to
Soaring Hawk's eyes and trickled down his cheeks and

into his mouth. He blinked his eyes against the blur, staring in sorrow at the dead animal, the bloody eyes staring back, piercing him, looking at the color of his heart.

It was a strange thing to have happened. Soaring Hawk was a hunter, and he had learned to kill game with care and with respect, not with sorrow. No man could bear the grief if he wept over every animal he had to kill. But there was something different, something important about this otter. In death its spirit had reached out and grabbed Soaring Hawk's heart and squeezed it painfully, leaving it blue and swollen against his throat.

It was impossible after that to cut the hide into strips for thongs. That would have been too degrading for so important an animal. So Soaring Hawk kept the skin whole and left the dark brown fur intact. He dressed and dried it himself and stored it away under his bed in the winter house. He knew in his heart that it was meant for something special. And now its special purpose was revealed. The otter skin was to be the symbol of Soaring Hawk's kinship with the river. By wearing it he would remind himself, and maybe others, that knowledge and power had gathered in his heart to change him, and that with the help of the river he had become a man, a curer who could stand in the world alone.

But how exactly could he *use* the skin? A man whom he had seen long ago at a New Corn Festival came to his mind. The man belonged to the Bird clan. He had come from upriver at Smoky Bluff Town. Hanging from his belt was a pouch made of a whole otter skin. He stayed in the homestead of Black Fox's people, and Soaring Hawk had seen him while visiting there. Though he was only a young boy at the time, he could still remember the fine otter pouch. He had never seen one like it before, nor had he since. The man with the pouch never came to another festival.

Something must have happened to him. Soaring Hawk had always meant to ask his father if something had.

Now his mind was made up. An otter pouch would be the perfect thing. He could use the whole skin, even the head could stay on. He could carry his pipe in it, and extra moccasins and parched corn when he went hunting. When he was curing, he could use it for a medicine bag and carry beads and gourd rattles and whatever else he might need. It would be simple to make. He would fold the tail end up almost to the head and sew up the sides. The head would fold down as a flap to close the pouch, and the legs would be left free to dangle. The tail would hang down the front looking as if it were being held in the otter's mouth, a very desirable effect, for if a real otter were actually to hold his tail in his mouth, he would have made himself into a circle, and circles were signs of great power.

Excited by the idea, Soaring Hawk jumped to his feet and hurried across the yard to the winter house where the otter skin was stored. Stooping low, he went in through the narrow passage that was the entranceway. Designed to keep out the wind, the winding entranceway also kept out the light, and but for the dim glow at the doorway, the inside was pitch black.

A small torch would have been helpful but it had seemed too much of a bother. After all, this was just a small room and Soaring Hawk knew it as well as he knew the fingers on his hand. But now remembering the snakes and spiders and other creepy things that sometimes find their way into the cool darkness of unused winter houses, he hung back in the light that spilled in from the outside. Suddenly it seemed a better idea to have a light, and he was on the verge of turning back to get one. But he was stopped by a challenge taking shape within him. Brave in the Light? Would that be his name? Was he so scared of his own winter house? The challenge was as real as if June Bug and Hard Mush were standing there chiding him.

He smiled. It was good to be pressed into doing

something brave. He stepped forward into the darkness, and suddenly he could see nothing. He could imagine snakes coiled on the floor, and big spiders hanging from the ceiling, and lizards scurrying about. He stood as still as a stone and held his breath. There was nothing. He made a noise with his foot, then listened again, and this time his heart raced as a light, crisp, scampering sound reached his ears. Lizards! And there were probably snakes and spiders as well. He looked behind at the soft light of the doorway, longing to turn back. But he scolded himself: The fear is in your head, you coward—you've been standing here building it up. What are a few lizards? Or even a harmless snake or two? All you have to do is walk across the room to your bed, pull out the basket under it, and take out the otter skin.

So he moved ahead, stepping quickly through the darkness until suddenly his foot cracked against something hard. He clenched his teeth as a sharp pain shot through him and then subsided. Groping in the dark, he found what must have been a hearthstone that someone had moved out of place, and he set it off to one side so as not to hit it again on the way out.

He went forward more slowly now, exploring the black space before him with first one foot and then the other until at last he came to his bed against the opposite wall. It was no trouble at all to find the basket and pull it out. He banged it against the floor a few times to encourage any creepy things to crawl out, then, cringing a bit at what he was afraid he might feel, he reached inside and jerked out the otter skin. He shook it hard, imaginary spiders crawling from it onto his arm. He thought he felt something on his shoulder, but when he brushed at it, his hand felt nothing. Then he thought he felt something on his head, then on the back of his leg.

He needed to be able to see! He wheeled around, and fixing his eyes on the light of the doorway, he hurried toward it through the darkness. Suddenly his bare foot came down on something soft and cool and strange. It moved. With a convulsive leap Soaring Hawk dove through the doorway. Scrambling to his feet, he ran the last few steps out into the bright sunshine and came to a shuddering halt.

Blinking and squinting in the brilliant light of day, as the screen of darkness faded from his eyes, he saw to his chagrin Chestnut Bread standing before him, and he knew that she had seen his ridiculous exit. She didn't speak but gave him instead a startled, questioning look.

"I tripped in the dark," he shrugged. "Someone left a hearthstone in the way."

"Did you go in there without a light?" she asked incredulously. "With all the creepy things that might be in there?"

Soaring Hawk looked at her hard. He could not tell if she were praising him for his bravery or laughing at his foolishness. It seemed best to forget the whole thing.

"Redbird will be glad to see you," he said and began to walk with her toward the summer house. "She has to stay inside until tomorrow. She needs some company, I think."

"Dark winter houses are always scary to me," Chestnut Bread persisted. "Once one of my fathers stepped right on top of a snake in his winter house."

Soaring Hawk stopped in his tracks. How could she know what he had just done? Maybe she was just guessing and was joking with him to find out. But she wasn't laughing, so maybe she wasn't joking at all.

"Which father was it? What did he do?"

"It was my screaming father," she said, as a smile spread across her face. "We call him that because when he stepped on the snake, he screamed. And that's the truth."

The two of them burst into laughter. Soaring Hawk's heart grew lighter and lighter until it soared like a bird toward the very top of the sky. It seemed to him that

they were the only two people in the world and that
they would always be together like this, sharing their
laughter.

But all at once Chestnut Bread grew serious. "I
shouldn't have told you that," she said softly. "He's my
father and I have great respect for him. The story is
true, but I call him father and I should not have told
it. I'm the one who is supposed to stand up for him
when other people make fun of him. We never call him
that name to his face or in front of outsiders. This father of mine is a very brave man. I'm ashamed that I
told you the story."

"You don't need to feel that way, Chestnut Bread."
He looked away from her because he had spoken her
name. "I'll never tell it to anyone. It will be as if I never
heard it."

Chestnut Bread looked at the ground without speaking.

"Don't you believe me?" he said. "I would rather die
than repeat that story. There's no need to be ashamed.
I think you are showing great respect for your father.
So if I swear not to tell the story, there's no harm to
anyone."

"Do you truly swear?" she asked.

"I truly swear."

She looked up and smiled. "It *is* a funny story to tell
about such a brave man." She began to chuckle again.

"Which father was it?" Soaring Hawk asked, trying
not to sound very interested. "Maybe you should call
him your brave father."

"There would be no point in that. If you think about
it, you'll realize that all my fathers are brave, and so if
I called him my brave father, people still wouldn't
know which one I meant. That's why I call him my
lucky hunter father, because everyone knows he's the
best hunter of all his brothers. I'm only telling you because you swore to me that it would be like you never
heard it."

Without looking at him again, Chestnut Bread

turned and walked quickly into the summer house.
Soaring Hawk stood for a moment trying to get control
of the smile that was sweeping across his face at the
thought of Big Buck yelling because he had stepped on
a snake. It was also pleasing to think that when he
himself had been in the same situation, he had shown
more courage. Admittedly he had jumped, but at least
he had not screamed.

As he moved toward the summer house, he began to
wonder about Chestnut Bread. What did she mean by
telling him that story? Was it only something she had
been reminded of because she had seen him come from
the winter house? Or had she been making fun of him
because she suspected that something in there had
scared him? Yet she made him feel brave instead of
foolish. Had she meant to? And why tell him that the
story was about one of her fathers? Since Big Buck was
a Wolf, it reflected badly on all the Wolf clan. Could it
be she was trying to say that she was on the Deer
people's side in the feud? That was possible, but he
could not be sure about it. It seemed that with her he
could not be sure about anything.

Neither Redbird nor Chestnut Bread nor Easy
Dancer looked around when Soaring Hawk came into
the summer house. "I knew you would hate to miss the
last of them," Chestnut Bread was saying, "so I stayed
longer and picked a few for you. I'm sorry there aren't
more."

Soaring Hawk's heart leaped as he saw her hand
large basket of blackberries to Easy Dancer. Two day
ago he had given her a rabbit to give to her clan moth
ers and now she was offering berries to his mother. D
she mean it as an exchange for the meat so that
would know to keep trying to win her? But if that
what she meant, she wasn't showing it. She sti
not even acknowledged his presence in the
Maybe it was nothing more than what she said
the time Redbird was able to go out again,
the berries would be gone.

Soaring Hawk was so exasperated from trying to understand her that he turned in a huff and strode stonily into the other room of the house. There he fumbled through several baskets trying to find an awl and enough length of sinew for sewing up his pouch. In the front room the women were laughing. He supposed they were laughing at him, and he clenched his teeth in anger.

Five

For the rest of the afternoon Soaring Hawk sat alone
on a cane mat in the shade of a tree and worked on his
otter skin pouch. As the day wore on, the breezes stiffened and clouds drifted in, building each upon the
other, growing darker and darker until the sky hung
heavy with the promise of rain.

"It looks like more than a thundershower," Black
Fox said at the evening meal.

"It looks like it might last all night," said Easy
Dancer.

"I guess it will be good for the corn," Redbird said.

"The corn has had enough rain," said Easy Dancer.
"I hope the squash doesn't rot."

Soaring Hawk was glad to see his sister in high spirits. But he gulped down his food without saying anything. His thoughts were on the evening. He was eager
to get to the square, where plans would be made for
the New Corn Festival. He wondered if they would
open the town house. If it did rain, it would be snug
and dry in the townhouse and there would be a special
feeling in the air, a closeness, a friendliness fed by rain
on the roof and soft memories. They would discuss the
festival for a while, making plans, and then someone
would begin a story, and everyone would sit back and
listen.

The evening light was fading behind heavy clouds as
Soaring Hawk reached the square. More people than
usual had turned out tonight. He made his way slowly
through the crowd looking for Hard Mush and June

Bug. He looked for Chestnut Bread, too, but with no
idea of what he would do if he saw her. He would not
want to add wood to the gossip fires by speaking to her
here at the square. But perhaps she would at least notice him and see things about him that pleased her.

"Hey, where did you get that funny-looking squirrel?" June Bug's voice called from behind.

Soaring Hawk turned with a grin, knowing now that
his otter pouch looked as beautiful as he had hoped.
"Where have you two been?" he asked. "I've been
looking everywhere."

"We've been over by the mound," said Hard Mush.
"Big Turtle sent Fisher to build up the fire in the townhouse. They're going to open it up so the rain won't
stop the planning for the festival."

"I'd been hoping for that," said Soaring Hawk.

"And so had everyone else," said June Bug. "Look
at all the people here tonight."

Hard Mush shook his head. "At the end of winter
everyone can hardly wait to move outside to the arbors
and danceground, but after they've been out for a
while, they all want to go back in."

"We heard that your sister is better," said June Bug.

"Yes, she's doing fine. It was never very serious."

"That's good to hear," said Hard Mush.

"Let's get over to the townhouse," said Soaring
Hawk. "They must be almost ready to let us in."

They began moving through the square, swaggering
a bit, looking at the girls who were walking around in
groups looking and laughing at the boys. Soaring Hawk
was feeling very handsome with his chickadee in his
hair and his otter on his belt. He wore no moccasins or
leggings with his breechcloth, but his feather cape was
hanging rakishly over one shoulder, and he wore his
best ear ornaments.

They worked their way through the crowd to the
townhouse mound. The last bit of light had given way
to black night, and now they glanced anxiously at the
sky. They could smell rain in the strong, gusty wind

and hear thunder rumbling low in the nearby mountains.

A drum sounded from atop the mound and a hush fell over the square as the people waited to hear the words of the town crier. From the top of the mound his voice came strong and clear: *"The townhouse is ready. The beloved men welcome you."*

A young man with a torch came from the townhouse and stood at the head of the steps. The flame whipped wildly in the wind, lighting the way for the people hurrying up the steep flight of steps. Huge drops began to fall, and by the time Soaring Hawk ducked inside the townhouse, water was already trickling down his neck.

It was dark inside, with only a small fire in the center of the great room, and Soaring Hawk could barely see. In the jostle of the crowd he lost June Bug and Hard Mush. He almost bumped into Scratcher, but he slipped away without being noticed and soon found his two friends, who had settled themselves to wait for the storytelling that was sure to come later.

As Soaring Hawk sat down beside them, Hard Mush said, "Look. There's a friend of yours."

He looked. There near the hearth stood Chestnut Bread, golden in the soft firelight. He caught his breath at the sight. "You mean a friend of my sister's," he murmured.

"A friend of yours, as I hear it. A blackberry friend."

Soaring Hawk clenched his teeth and silently cursed the gossipers, who never seemed to miss a thing. "My *sister's* blackberry friend. She brought them to Redbird."

"That's not the way I heard it."

"That's the way *I* heard it," said June Bug. "My sister was with her when she picked them. She said they were for Redbird."

Soaring Hawk was grateful to June Bug. It was Hard Mush's way to keep pushing until a person was thoroughly miserable. But June Bug was more sensitive; he understood the hearts of others and seemed always to know the limits of a friendly joke.

"It would seem she would have a hard time being the friend of anyone in the Deer homestead," said Hard Mush. "She stays so much with Scratcher's wives. She's always at their homestead, eating from the same food pot as Scratcher."

"It is not the Paint clan that is in the feud," said Soaring Hawk.

"But Scratcher is one of her fathers. Surely she has respect for her fathers."

"Of course she has."

"Then why does she go so often to your homestead? Perhaps she's Scratcher's spy."

Soaring Hawk felt a surge of anger.

"Redbird is like her sister," June Bug reminded Hard Mush. "A feud is a passing thing. Someday it will be over and forgotten. But the hearts of sisters cling together forever."

"That is well said, brother," said Soaring Hawk.

"I hope you are right about an end to the feud," said Hard Mush. "From what I've been hearing, it won't be over very soon."

"What have you heard?" asked Soaring Hawk.

"I heard my father talking with his brothers today. They said Scratcher is speaking against your uncle again."

"What is he saying?"

"That perhaps your uncle is not such a powerful man after all since he can't seem to keep your sister from getting ill, and . . . well, and things such as that."

"What things such as that?"

"It doesn't really matter, brother."

"Yes it does. What else did he say? What else is supposed to show weakness in my uncle?"

Hard Mush looked to June Bug for help.

"Your hunting," June Bug said quietly.

Soaring Hawk fumed with anger. "That? He is

spreading that across the town? It is my affair, my own personal affair! It has nothing to do with my uncle!"

"People know that," said June Bug. "Your hunting is only bad luck. Everyone has a little bad luck now and then."

"Like our friend here," said Hard Mush, nodding toward June Bug. "The champion chunky player."

Soaring Hawk had to smile. June Bug laughed and the tension broke. They turned their conversation to lighter things, relaxing again in familiar companionship, three friends who were as close as brothers. Their hearts too would cling together forever.

The evening passed quickly. With the women on one side of the room and the men on the other, the festival plans were made amid arguments and laughter. Problems of the last festival were discussed, and the assignment of tasks for the coming event was begun. After a while, the discussions came slowly to a halt and people began to sit back, talking softly among themselves, waiting for the storytelling to begin. Soon, the room grew quiet, and Big Turtle, the most beloved of the old men, began a strange and beautiful story which Soaring Hawk found all the more wonderful on this stormy ___, here among his people, in the old townhouse.

" 'hunder lives in the west," Big Turtle began, "near the place where the sun goes down behind the water. In the old times he sometimes made a journey to the east, and once after he had come back from one of these journeys, a child was born in the east who, the people said, was his son. As the boy grew up it was found that he had terrible sores all over his body, so one day his mother said to him, 'Your father, Thunder, is a great medicine man. He lives far to the west, but if you find him he can cure you.'

"So the boy set out to find his father and be cured. He traveled long toward the west, asking of everyone he met where Thunder lived, until at last they began to tell him that it was only a little way ahead. He went on and came to a place on the Tenasi River where a man called Copper lived. Now Copper was a great gambler, and it was he who invented the chunky game that we play with a wheel and pole. He challenged everyone who came by to play against him. Copper won almost every time he played because he was so tricky, and so his house had been filled with all kinds of fine things. Sometimes he would lose, and then he would bet all that he had, including his own life, but the winner got nothing for his trouble, for Copper knew how to take on different shapes, so that he always got away.

"As soon as Copper saw the boy, he asked him to stop and play awhile, but the boy said he was looking for his father, Thunder, and could not stop. 'Well,' said Copper, 'he lives nearby; you can hear him grumbling over there all the time, so we may as well have a game or two before you go on.' The boy said he had nothing to bet. 'That's all right,' said the gambler, 'we'll play for your pretty spots.' He said this to make the boy angry so he would play, but still the boy said he must go and find his father, and would come back afterward.

"The boy went on and came at last to Thunder's house. Thunder asked him why he had come. 'I have sores all over my body, and my mother told me you were my father and a great medicine man, and if I came here you would cure me.'

"'Yes,' said the father, 'I am a great medicine man, and I will cure you.'

"So Thunder healed the sores on his son's skin. Then Thunder's wife took the boy aside and told him this: 'Your father will now want to put some new clothes on you, but when he opens his box and tells you to pick out your ornaments, be sure to take them from the bottom. Then he will send for his other sons to play ball against you. There is a honey-locust tree in front of the house, and as soon as you begin to get tired, strike at that. Your father will then stop the play, because he does not want to lose the tree.'

"They went back to Thunder, who then said to the boy, 'Now we must dress you.' He brought out some fine clothes of buckskin and had the boy put them on. Then he opened a box and said, 'Now pick out your necklace and bracelets.'

"The boy looked and the box was full of all kinds of snakes gliding over each other with their heads up. Remembering what the woman had told him, he was not afraid. He plunged his hand to the bottom and drew out a great rattlesnake and put it around his neck for a necklace. He put down his hand again four times and drew up four copperheads and twisted them around his wrists and ankles. Then his father gave him a war club and said, 'Now you must play a ball game with your two elder brothers. They live beyond here in the Darkening Land, and I have sent for them.'

"Thunder said a ball game, but he meant that the boy must fight for his life. The young men came, and they were both older and stronger than the boy, but he was not afraid and fought against them. The thunder rolled and the lightning flashed at every stroke, for they were the two Thunder Boys, and the boy himself was Lightning. At last he was tired from defending himself alone against two, and he pretended to aim a blow at the honey-locust tree. Then Thunder stopped the fight because he was afraid the lightning would split the tree, and he saw that the boy was brave and strong. We know this is true because even today lightning never strikes a honey-locust tree.

"The boy now told his father how Copper had dared him to play chunky with him, and had even offered to play for the sores on his skin. 'Yes,' said Thunder, 'he is a great gambler, but I will see that you win. Go back the way you came, and as soon as he sees you, he will challenge you to play. He is very hard to beat, but this time he will lose every game. He will bet everything he has until at last he will bet his life, and lose. Then send at once for your brothers to kill him, or he will get away, he is so tricky.'

"Everything happened as Thunder said it would. Copper played until he lost everything he had and at last he even staked his life. But though he lost the game, he was too sly for the boy and got away before he could be killed. The boy ran to his father's house and got his brothers to help him. They brought their dog—the Horned Green Beetle—and hurried after the gambler as fast as they could. After a while they met an old woman making pottery and asked her if she had seen Copper. She said she had not. 'He came this way,' said the brothers.

" 'Then he must have passed in the night,' said the old woman, 'for I have been here all day.' They were about to take another path when the Beetle, who had been circling about in the air above the old woman, made a dart at her and struck her on the forehead, and it rang like copper. Then they knew it was Copper and sprang at him, but he jumped up in his right shape and was off running so fast that he was soon out of sight again. The Beetle had struck so hard that some of the copper rubbed off, and we can still see it on the beetle's forehead today.

"They followed and came to an old man sitting by the trail, carving a stone pipe. They asked him if he had seen Copper pass that way. He said no, but again the Beetle, who could know Copper under any shape, struck him on the forehead so that it rang like metal, and the gambler jumped up in his right form and was off again before they could hold him. He ran east until he came to the great water; then he ran north until he came to the edge of the world and had to turn again to the west. He took every shape to throw them off the track, but the Beetle always knew him, and the brothers pressed him so hard that at last he could go no more, and they caught him just as he reached the edge of the great water where the sun goes down.

"They tied his hands and feet with a grapevine and drove a long stake through his breast, and they planted it far out in the deep water. They set two crows on the end of the pole to guard it and called the place 'Crow Place.' But Copper never died and cannot die until the end of the world. He lies there in the water with his face always turned up. Sometimes he struggles to get free, and sometimes the beavers, who are his friends, come and gnaw at the grapevine to release him. Then the pole shakes and the crows at the top cry, 'Caw! Caw! Caw!' and scare the beavers away."

Big Turtle had finished, and there was a long silence while people thought about the story and the wonder of it. Then a hum of quiet talk took hold and grew, and soon there was loud talking and then cheers went up as Bent Nose stepped out and began to tell another story. His was followed by another, and that one by another, and the night grew old before all the people went home.

Six

The downpour that caught Soaring Hawk on the way home from the townhouse soaked him to the skin. He ducked into the summer house and found it dark and everyone asleep. Shedding his wet clothes, he stepped near the hearth's embers and wondered how he could find something warm to wrap up in without waking everybody.

"There's a blanket by your foot," whispered a voice so close to him he jumped. It was Fighting Bear. Soaring Hawk peered through the darkness. He could barely make out his uncle's dark form lying on the other side of the hearth.

"Did the rain catch you?" whispered Soaring Hawk.

"Yes. Your mother wouldn't let me go home."

Soaring Hawk reached down and found the blanket, and when he picked it up, a breechcloth fell to the floor. A blanket and a dry breechcloth. Someone had been thinking of him. Someone knew he would be coming home cold and wet and had wanted to make it better. With a grateful heart he wondered who it was. He would never think of asking. In the morning he would thank whoever it was by announcing that he had gone to sleep dry and warm last night. That would be enough. The person being thanked would know. Probably it was Easy Dancer—or maybe Fighting Bear. Wrapping himself in the blanket, he laid down contentedly by the fire.

"How were things at the townhouse?" Fighting Bear asked softly.

"Good," whispered Soaring Hawk. "At first everyone was talking about the festival, but then people started telling stories."

"Which stories?"

"The funniest was about how the possum got his bare tail. Fisher told it."

Fighting Bear chuckled quietly. "He tells that one well, doesn't he?"

"Yes, and he was really good tonight. But the story I liked best was the one Big Turtle told about Thunder's son and Copper. There was a part in it where Thunder's son reached right down to the bottom of a box of snakes. I really liked that story."

"It's a good one," said Fighting Bear. "A person who wants to know things should listen to stories like that and think about them."

They lay in silence. Soaring Hawk's thoughts drifted to the crows that were left by the Thunder Boys to stand guard over the great water. Crows flapping their wings to scare away the beavers. It was a strange job for crows. Usually people were standing guard to scare crows away. Soaring Hawk used to do it, when he was little, when it was his turn to guard the fields. He was good at scaring away the crows. The old grandfathers that watched with him told him so. He was good back then. Back when he was little. . . . Soaring Hawk drifted into sleep. He slept heavily at first, then fitfully, then he was struggling to wake up, trying to get away from a dream. He opened his eyes, his heart beating fast. He looked for the fire and found the coals still glowing. Having something in the dark to look at helped him feel awake, and made the terror of his dream begin to fade.

It was a strange dream. He had been walking toward the square and had seen Hard Mush and June Bug playing a game of chunky. They were the only two on the yard. No one was in the arbors or anywhere around. As he drew closer, it suddenly began to rain, and he saw that the bracelets on his friends' arms had turned to rattlesnakes and their necklaces to copperheads. They seemed not to notice. Soaring Hawk had wanted to call out a warning, but when they turned toward him, he saw that they were not his friends after all, but two boys he had never seen before, strange boys with a wild look about them, who were motioning for him to come near. He tried to turn and run, but his feet kept taking him closer and closer to them until he could see scales on the snakes and tongues shooting in and out. The strange boys watched him with faces that were wild and laughing. At that point, he could stand it no more and he forced himself awake.

Such a dream was not one to be forgotten. The two strangers must have been Thunder people, perhaps the two Thunder Boys themselves. He would have to mention it to Fighting Bear in the morning to see what he thought it meant.

It was hard to go back to sleep. Whenever he shut his eyes, the dream began to come back. So Soaring Hawk lay staring at the hearth, trying to think of lighter things to put his mind at ease. Just as he was beginning to feel drowsy, he heard the cry of an owl—a night-goer owl! He sat up. Was it an owl or was it a night-goer? He fixed his eyes on the doorway. If the mat hanging there made the slightest movement, he would call for Fighting Bear. He listened, but the owl cried no more. Perhaps it had gone away. He began to relax.

Suddenly it happened! The mat was pulled back and a dark form was standing in the doorway. Soaring Hawk leaped to his feet, his heart pounding in his ears. But before he could call out, the figure spoke in a hushed and familiar voice: "Take it easy, Nephew. What makes you so jumpy?"

Soaring Hawk sank back to his blanket in relief. "Didn't you hear the night-goer owl?"

"Yes," said Fighting Bear. "It only called once. Then I scared it away."

"What do you think it was?"

"Probably just an owl. But you never can be sure."

"I didn't know you were outside."

"I woke up from a bad dream," said Fighting Bear, settling down on his side of the hearth. "I went out to clear my head. The rain has stopped."

Soaring Hawk wondered what Fighting Bear had dreamed. There were so many bad signs filling the night that he heaved a weary sigh as he turned on his side to sleep.

"My dream concerned you, so you might as well hear it," Fighting Bear said quietly.

Soaring Hawk rolled back over. "I'm listening," he said.

"It was a short dream, but it was long in meaning. I dreamed I was sleeping here in this house. Everyone was home but you, just as it was earlier tonight. In my dream I woke up to find the house on fire. Fire covered the door, and there was no way for us to escape. But then I saw through the flames to the yard outside and there you were battling the blaze. I knew then that everything was up to you, that you were the only one who could put it out."

Soaring Hawk lay still, almost without breathing.

"It was an important dream," Fighting Bear added. "Do you know the meaning?"

"Yes," whispered Soaring Hawk. "It means that someone in the house is going to fall ill, and it will be up to me to make the cure." He spoke in a calm voice, but his thoughts were racing in his head. When would it happen? Who would be the one to fall ill? How ill?

"Did I put the fire out?" he asked.

"I don't know. I woke up too soon. You should get some sleep now. We'll talk about it in the morning."

But Soaring Hawk could not sleep, not with his mind jumping around like a grasshopper in a gourd bottle. Perhaps he dozed a time or two, but never for very long. When the rim of night lightened ever so slightly around the mat in the doorway, he was awake to see it. Rising quietly from his blanket, he went outside.

The clouds had disappeared and moonlight lay gently on the misty earth. In the east the stars were dim, and Soaring Hawk knew that it was morning. He breathed deeply the good smell of wet earth and leaves and wood. A few whippoorwills still called through the darkness, but they fell silent one by one, and the birds of the day began to waken. In the beauty of the morning he felt strong and renewed, no longer worried about Fighting Bear's dream. It was likely that the dream was nothing more than a comment on what had already happened. After all, this was the morning that he would finish Redbird's cure. She was the member of the household who had fallen ill, and he had been the one to cure her.

As the light grew in the east, Soaring Hawk could hear the family waking up. His spirits were high now, and after one more deep breath of morning air, he went back inside the summer house. He found Easy Dancer already up and about and Fighting Bear sitting on his blanket rubbing his crippled leg.

"Is your leg all right?" asked Soaring Hawk.

"I think so," said Fighting Bear. "You know how it is—slow to get going some mornings. Especially when it rains."

"The sky is clear now," said Soaring Hawk. "It's going to be nice today."

Redbird was still sleeping soundly in her bed, her face to the wall. Easy Dancer went over and shook her gently, saying, "Time to wake up." Redbird lay still. Easy Dancer waited a moment and then said, "Come on now." Still there was no response. Chuckling at her laziness, Easy Dancer shook her harder. "Come on, Daughter. We can't start the cure without you, you know." Redbird stirred but did not roll over. Easy Dancer waited a moment longer. "Redbird!" she then said sharply. "Your mother is speaking to you. I'll not tell you again." She turned away, expecting to have to say no more.

Soaring Hawk watched Redbird with growing uneasiness. "Sister," he said at last, "are you all right?"

Easy Dancer turned back in sudden bewilderment. They leaned over Redbird and found that she was awake, staring at the wall. She allowed them to turn her over, but she did not look at them, and stared instead at the ceiling.

"What's wrong, Sister?" asked Soaring Hawk. "Tell us what is wrong." She answered by turning her face to the wall.

Soaring Hawk heard a grunt and looked around to see Fighting Bear abandoning an effort to stand. "Come give me a hand, Nephew," he said. "I don't know what's wrong with this leg."

"I'll help you, Brother-in-Law," said Black Fox, who was coming from the other room to see what was wrong with his daughter. He pulled Fighting Bear to his feet, and Fighting Bear leaned heavily on him as they moved to Redbird's side. Soaring Hawk held out his walking stick, but Fighting Bear waved it away.

"Find me a place to sit down. I don't know what's wrong with this leg. I've got to get off it altogether." Soaring Hawk cleared a seat next to Redbird, and Fighting Bear sat down with a grunt. He leaned over Redbird and said, "Can you hear me, Niece?"

She didn't answer.

"You must speak to me if you can. Can you hear me?"

"Yes," said Redbird. Her voice was strange, as if it came from far away.

"Are you in pain?" asked Fighting Bear.

There was no answer.

"Do you ache?" he asked.

"Yes," she said in the same strange voice.

"In your stomach?" he asked.

"Yes."

"In your head?"

"Yes."

"In your arms?"

"Yes."

"Do you ache all over then?" he asked.

"Yes," she said, and once again she turned her face away. Fighting Bear felt her cheek. It was hot.

"Did you dream last night?" he asked.

"No," she murmured.

Fighting Bear gave a sigh. "Help me up, Nephew," he said. "We must go out and talk." He reached over and put his hand on Easy Dancer's arm. "Don't worry, Sister. Your daughter will be all right."

Outside, at Fighting Bear's insistence, they went no farther than the big oak tree, and there Soaring Hawk helped ease him to the ground. He had never seen Fighting Bear's leg bother him so much; and he had never seen his sister so sick. "Things are looking bad," he said as he sat down beside his uncle.

"Very bad," said Fighting Bear. "The things my dream spoke of are already upon us. I never thought it would be so soon."

"How do we know that's what it is?" asked Soaring Hawk. "Why can't *you* cure Redbird?"

"With this leg?" There was despair in Fighting Bear's voice. "I couldn't even walk to the river with this leg. No, Nephew, we have been warned in my dream that this cure is yours, and a medicine man must always listen to what the forces of the world are telling him. Perhaps the leg is a further warning."

"It's conjury," muttered Soaring Hawk. "Someone has done this to us. I think I know who it is."

"Don't be too hasty," warned Fighting Bear. "If it is conjury, then you must be sure to name the right person or else be powerless against him. To name the right person, you have to depend on what you know. That is why you must always have your eyes open when you walk through the town or stop at the square, and that is why you should always listen to all the things people are saying. To know a conjurer, you have to know the affairs of the people and the color of each person's heart."

"I hear what you're telling me," said Soaring Hawk. "I *have* been watching and listening, and that's why I know who it is. It is Scratcher. He's the one who made you embarrass him last year in the matter of the rain. It was his fault, but he blames you, and he hasn't tried at all to hide his red heart. And lately he's been doing things that make me even more suspicious." Soaring Hawk told about the incident by the river and the meeting with Chestnut Bread in the path and about the things his friends had told him in the townhouse.

"Well, Scratcher or not, the situation does look like conjury," said Fighting Bear. "Redbird was healthy and happy when she went to bed, but now she's feverish and so despondent and blue that she won't even look at us. So perhaps it is conjury. What are you going to do about it?"

"Me?" asked Soaring Hawk, caught slightly off guard. He still could not believe that he was going to have to do it all alone. "I guess I'll go to the river and try to work against him."

"You *guess* you'll *try*?" said Fighting Bear scornfully.

Soaring Hawk felt ashamed. He drew his shoulders up. "I'll go inside and prepare myself," he said, making his voice sound as forceful and resolute as he could. "I'll put the chickadee in my hair to help me know the truth, and I'll wear my otter pouch to help me draw power from the river. Then I'll follow the river until I come to a secluded place that looks upstream toward the Sun Land. I'll conjure there against our enemy until I've won this battle and turned the curse back upon the sender. Then my beloved sister will be well, and my beloved uncle will walk again without pain. Until these things are accomplished, I shall not return to my people."

"Those are good words, Nephew. Well spoken. You say you will wear the chickadee. That is good. In the chickadee you will have power from the Upper World where belong the birds and all flying things and all the noblest of the powerful beings, the ones we so seldom see. And you say you will wear the otter, and that is also good. In the otter you will have the power of the Under World, the power of the snakes and reptiles, the things in the water and in the mountains, and all the most terrifying of the powerful beings. But you are not complete, Nephew. You have nothing from This World to give you the power of the four-legged animals, and of men, and of all the forces and spirits that are closest to us. Go inside for me and get my pouch. It is near the hearth where I slept last night."

Soaring Hawk did as he was asked, and when Fighting Bear got the pouch, he took from it a long-stemmed pipe and handed it to Soaring Hawk. "Now you are complete," he said.

Soaring Hawk was speechless. It was Fighting Bear's bear pipe, the one old Owl had made. It was carved from soapstone. Never had there been a pipe more exquisitely crafted. On the stem facing the smoker a miniature bear was perched. The little stone figure seemed to be snarling a warning. It was a mother bear protecting her cub, for there *was* a cub, behind her, climbing up the bowl of the pipe. The beauty of the pipe was in these two bears so wonderously carved that they seemed to have a life of their own.

It was the finest gift Soaring Hawk had ever received. He turned to speak his feelings, but he could not find words to say enough. He turned back in silence and slipped the pipe into his belt.

"Let's go inside," said Fighting Bear.

Soaring Hawk rose and helped Fighting Bear to his feet, then supported him as they made their way slowly to the summer house. Once there, he eased Fighting Bear down by the fire, then went into the other room, leaving it to his uncle to explain things.

Sitting on a bunk with his head in his hands, Soaring Hawk listened. He could hear Fighting Bear explaining everything, and he could hear the silence of his mother and father. His chest tightened; his breathing became shallow and quick. His hands grew sweaty. How could he do it? How could he go out there alone and do everything right? He had never worked at the river alone. Fighting Bear had always been there, even if only to hold the beads. He squeezed his eyes shut in despair. Why had he never learned to handle the beads? He should have practiced. Why had he always let Fighting Bear do it? It was the beads moving under their own power that told who was winning and who was not. He could not work without them. Someone was going to have to go with him. Someone who could handle the beads.

Soaring Hawk jumped to his feet and strode into the room where his family and his father were sitting. "Uncle," he blurted out, "in your dream did you see anyone outside helping me fight the fire?"

"No," said Fighting Bear. "I saw only you."

"Could there have been someone you didn't see?"

"Yes, I suppose so. What have you got on your mind, Nephew? You know this has to be your own cure."

"It will be mine," said Soaring Hawk. "But why couldn't I take an assistant? Someone to handle the beads."

"Who would go? How could you ask someone who knows more than you to come to be your assistant?"

"I don't know, but I'd like to try it anyway. It would even be good to have someone who knows more than Scratcher."

"What about Owl?" said Easy Dancer. "He knows more than anyone."

"He's an old man," said Fighting Bear. "He stays to himself."

"Yes," she said, "but he's always liked you, ever since he healed your wounds from the bear fight. I think he would help us because Soaring Hawk is your nephew."

"He might," said Fighting Bear. "But if Soaring Hawk is to have an assistant, he must choose his own."

Soaring Hawk paused uncertainly. He was afraid of Owl. He could not imagine himself walking up to the old man and asking him to be his assistant. But Easy Dancer was right. The old man was more powerful than anyone.

"I'll go ask Owl," he heard himself say.

Seven

Owl lived far out on the other side of town. Too far out, most people thought. Why would an old man want to live alone like that, so far away from family and friends? He had not always lived there. Once his homestead had been in the middle of town, near the square. He was head medicine man then and was loved and respected by everyone. Those were good times, people said. The crops seldom failed and hunting was always good. Disputes were settled without bloodshed and everyone was white and happy. They said it was because Owl knew so much, because he was such a powerful head medicine man.

Then one summer at the New Corn Festival Owl stood before the people and said that he was an old man now, he was tired, and it was time for him to step aside. They had cried out for him to keep his office, but when it was apparent he could not be dissuaded, the people chose Wren's Nest to take his place.

Directly after the festival Owl left the village unexpectedly. His relatives worried, and they went to their clansmen in nearby towns and asked about him, but no one had seen a trace of the old man. Finally, after sixteen days, Owl returned to the village. He was gaunt, as if he had been fasting, and there was a terrible exhaustion in his face as if he had been engaged in some great struggle.

His relatives ran to greet him, asking where he had been and what had happened to him. But he waved away their questions. "I am back," he said. "I am well. That is all that matters. Now let me rest."

No one would ask him about it after that, and the old man volunteered nothing. Indeed, he no longer talked very much about anything. He seldom came to the square. He just sat in the yard of his nieces' homestead and carved things from wood and stone and threw rocks at the dogs that ran into the garden.

Finally Owl surprised everyone by announcing that he was moving out of his nieces' homestead. It was the homestead of his lineage: He had grown up there, left there when he married, and returned again when his wife died. Now he said he was leaving once more. No one could convince him otherwise. When he told his relatives where he wanted to live, they objected, saying he would be too far away from them and anyone else who could be of help. But Owl had insisted, and so they built him a summer house and a winter house and a granary, and they left him alone.

People shook their heads, not knowing what to make of it. A few blamed it on his relatives, saying they had somehow mistreated the old man. But most people said no, something had changed him while he was away, something had happened to him, and they all wondered what it could have been.

Soaring Hawk was only a small boy when Owl had gone on his mysterious journey. But the stories circulated through the years and Soaring Hawk had heard them every one. There were two widely held though somewhat conflicting theories about Owl's peculiar behavior. One was that he had captured an ulunsuti crystal.

An ulunsuti was a marvelous seer's crystal that could only be obtained from the forehead of a great uktena, a giant serpent monster with antlers like a deer and wings like a bird. Uktenas lurked in high mountain passes and were more dangerous than anything else in the world. The ulunsuti on an uktena's forehead blazed like a brilliant star, giving off such bright flashes of light that anyone who looked upon it was so blinded and confused by it that he would run straight toward the monster and certain death. Only very rarely was there a person powerful and wise enough to kill an uktena, and if he did, the ulunsuti crystal would be his.

With an ulunsuti crystal a person could be successful in everything. His crops would never fail, and he would always find game; his wives would never be unfaithful, and his cures would always work; and by gazing into the ulunsuti, the owner of the marvelous crystal could see events before they actually took place. Yet this powerful object was also fraught with danger. Except for the owner, anyone coming near the ulunsuti would sicken and die, and the owner himself was in danger if he did not feed the crystal regularly by rubbing it with the warm blood of a freshly killed animal.

If a man as old as Owl had an ulunsuti, people reasoned, he would not want to keep it hidden away in a cave somewhere because then he would have to walk too far to feed it or use it. No, old Owl would want to keep his ulunsuti close at hand. That was why he moved away. It was to protect his family and friends from the dangerous ulunsuti that he wanted to hide in some secret part of his winter house. The people who thought Owl had an ulunsuti were supported in their belief by persistent reports of flashes of light from the old man's winter house, especially during thunderstorms, the very time an ulunsuti crystal would be most active.

But other people would insist it was only lightning. Owl has no ulunsuti, they would say. Not in his winter house, not in a cave, not anywhere. He is an old man, sure enough. But he was old even fifteen years ago, when he stepped aside as head medicine man. But he is a man who is only old in years. His legs are not old. They move briskly and easily and carry him far. He is often seen a morning's walk from home, and now and then a hunter will see him several days away. How does such an old man walk so far and all alone? Why are his hands not aching and tired like the crippled, arthritic hands of other old people? He still carves wood

and even soapstone, and his figures are always beautiful and exact, every part perfect. How can old hands
do that? How can old eyes see so well?

Before he went away that time, these people said,
Owl was growing old like anybody else. But since then
nothing about him has changed. Perhaps he gets a little
thinner, a little more wrinkled, a little more bent. But
that is simply to mislead us, to make us think he truly
is growing old so that we will not suspect he has become a night-goer.

Yes, these people said, Owl let his power carry him
too far. He did the most hateful and wicked thing a
person can do. He spent those sixteen days alone in the
woods where he fasted and drank the brew of the plant
that turns a person into a night-goer. Now he can
change himself into anything he chooses and go lurking
about the night in search of sick, helpless people whose
lives he can wrench away and add to his own.

That is why he is not growing old, they said. That is
why he moved away from other people and comes so
seldom to the square. A night-goer is spiteful and unnatural. He hates people. He would rather sit alone
than be in the company of his fellow men. Owl is still
friendly with the beloved old men, but that is only to
fool them, to make them not believe the others when
he is accused of being a night-goer. And why is he so
nice to the little children? Why, to win their trust so
that if he ever finds them alone they will come to him.
The poor little things would not even realize that while
patting their heads he would be stealing their livers,
and with their livers he would be stealing the long
years ahead that should have been theirs. That is why
these people warn the children to watch out for him.

Soaring Hawk felt weak inside. When he was younger he would run away at the very sight of old Owl.
Even after he had grown too old to run away, he still
could not bear to meet Owl alone on the path, and
whenever he saw the old man walking toward him, he

would always pretend that he had business in another direction.

Soaring Hawk was not really sure which of the stories about Owl he believed. Sometimes he was sure that Owl was a night-goer. There was the story Fisher told, for instance, about the time he was passing by Owl's homestead in the very early morning when there was still some darkness left in the sky. Fisher saw a big bird flying low. It was a night-goer owl, and it flew to Owl's summer house and lit on the roof. Then Fisher watched in horror as the owl walked over to the smoke hole and crawled right down inside the house. He was sure that the bird was the old man himself coming home from an evil night's work.

Anyone could tell by his face that Fisher was not lying about this, and the beloved old men never said he was. What they said was that the early morning light can trick a man's eyes. They also said that if the bird were the old man, then it made no sense for him to go into the summer house on a freezing winter morning, which was the kind of morning it had been. After long deliberation, the beloved old men said they were unwilling to accuse Owl of so horrible a crime on such dubious evidence. Many people shook their heads over that decision. "You expect night-goers to do things backward," they muttered. "It would be just like one to use the summer house in winter."

As Soaring Hawk left the last homestead behind, he wished he had not remembered Fisher's story. He tried to stay calm by telling himself that his own mother and uncle would not send him into the clutches of a wicked night-goer.

But his heart continued to fill with misgivings and his feet came slowly to a halt. The sun was rising over the mountains and he looked to it for courage. This was for Redbird, he reminded himself. He had never seen her so ill. He would walk beyond the streams to the Under World for her, so what was it to walk to Owl's house?

He moved forward again, quickening his pace, trying to take advantage of this small bit of courage he had been able to summon. Before he knew it he was on the path that led to Owl's homestead, and with hardly a pause he turned and strode boldly toward the old man's yard. How does such an old man keep such a big garden, he wondered, noticing the tall corn on either side of the path. He wished he had not thought of that, for too many answers came to mind, especially the one about night-goers only *looking* old. His knees weakened, but it was too late now to turn back.

The yard lay before him, and except for a dog that barked at him from the summer house door, it was deserted. He hoped for a moment that the old man was away, but he knew that was not the case—he had already seen the wisp of smoke from the roof. He stopped beside the cold fireplace in the yard and watched the mat that hung in the doorway of the summer house. He wanted Owl to come outside so they could talk in the morning light in full view of the path. Surely the dog's barking would bring the old man out.

"Hush, dog!" came a voice from inside; and then, "Come in, Grandchild. Come in." The dog skulked away as Soaring Hawk moved forward and slipped around the mat into the semi-darkness of the summer house. At first he could see almost nothing in the dim light, and though he knew the old man could see him, he could not decide which of the dark forms in the room he should be looking at. None of them moved.

"I've been expecting you, Grandchild," said the voice from the shadows.

Then all at once there was a whir of wings and the cry of an owl, and with a yell Soaring Hawk threw his arms about his head as a large bird swept against him and out the door.

He leaned weakly against the doorway, his trembling arms clutched against his chest and belly. Perhaps his heart and liver were gone. How could he know? If he died, he would know. He closed his eyes and tried to catch his breath. He could feel his heart now; it was still there pounding in his chest. There was reassurance in that at least. Perhaps old Owl had done nothing more than scare him half to death. He had to leave, had to get out of there before the old man came flying back to finish him off. He would go to the square and tell the elders that Fisher was right, that Owl really was a night-goer. He would do that now, right away. But as he turned to go, a soft chuckle came floating from a far corner of the room.

"My, my. Nobody seems to like that owl but me."

Soaring Hawk wheeled around and peered toward the voice. His eyes could see now. There just beyond the glow of the fire sat the old man, wrapped in a deer skin and sipping from a gourd bowl. Soaring Hawk sniffed the air. Sassafras tea.

"Why don't you fasten back that mat, Grandchild," the old man said. "Then come have a seat and use your head about night-goers and owls. In the first place, night-goers go about at night, just as the name tells us. Now surely you could not have failed to notice that this is morning, not night. Are you thinking about it? Now in the second place, a night-goer must be either one form or another. Since I am sitting here before you, I could not have just flown out the door." Owl chuckled again at the thought of it. "Of course," he added, "if I were an owl I might fly out the door and up to the roof, come back in the smoke hole, and change myself back before you knew it. And in fact, that's what the owl will probably do any time now, though he won't change into anything when he gets inside. No, Grandchild, I'm afraid an owl is all he is and all he ever will be. You startled him. We don't get many visitors, you know. But he'll be back."

Soaring Hawk hesitated. There was something about the old man's manner that was alluring, that made him want to go sit near him and have some sassafras tea. But on the other hand, he was wary of a trap. Why should he believe that the old man had a pet owl? Who had ever heard of such a thing?

He fastened back the mat as Owl had asked, and the morning light pushed back the shadows of the room. He glanced up at the smoke hole. If the owl came back so that he could see both the bird and Owl at the same time, then he would believe the old man's story.

He waited nervously by the door, glancing back and forth between Owl and the smoke hole. Owl sat quietly and the room filled with an uncomfortable silence. Soaring Hawk was casting about for something to say, anything to fill the unpleasant void, when the old man raised his bony hand and said, "Don't speak. You'll scare him away. He's coming in now."

Soaring Hawk looked up to see the owl crawl inside the smoke hole, pulling itself along with its beak. Once inside it flew over to a rafter in the darkest corner of the room. It looked about for a moment with big round eyes, then closed them one at a time, and with what seemed to be a weary sigh hunched down in its feathers to sleep. Soaring Hawk found himself smiling.

"It is good to see you," said Owl, as if Soaring Hawk had just entered the room. "Let me see—you are the boy who is always going someplace else. Easy Dancer's son, I believe, nephew of Fighting Bear. Come over to the fire, Grandchild. Have some tea."

Soaring Hawk went over and sat cross-legged at the hearth while Owl poured hot tea into the bowl. In his nervousness he found it difficult to think of anything to say. At last he asked rather foolishly, "Did you enjoy the rain last night?"

Owl passed him the tea. "Yes," he said, "it was pleasant. There was coolness in it, a promise of autumn. Of course, we will have hot days again. But summer has come halfway and more. I love the autumn season, don't you? I love it as much as spring. Maybe more. . . ."

As Owl rambled on about the weather and the seasons, Soaring Hawk stared nervously at the fire. He could feel his stomach knotting. It was not that he was afraid of Owl, not anymore. It was that he was in awe of him. He was suddenly struck by his own audacity. How could he have come here like this? Compared to Owl as a medicine man, Soaring Hawk was a newborn babe who had just jumped down from the mother's womb. How could he ask this powerful old man to come be his *assistant*? He must have been crazy even to think of it. Fighting Bear had warned him. Why had he not listened? What could he say now to Owl? What could he say now that he was sitting by his inside fire and drinking his tea?

"And how is your mother?" asked the old man. Soaring Hawk looked up, startled, wondering when the subject had changed from the weather.

"She is doing fine, Grandfather. Just fine." He sipped the tea uneasily, then passed the bowl back to Owl.

"And how about Fighting Bear? And your sister? Yours is not much of a lineage, you know, but I've always felt there was quality there."

"Thank you, Grandfather. I'm afraid my uncle is not too well today. His leg gives him great pain because my sister is very ill. You see, that's why—"

"Wait, now, wait. You are telling me that your uncle's leg is bad because your sister is sick?"

"That's right," said Soaring Hawk. He felt flustered and stupid, but there was nothing to do but go ahead. "It's like this, Grandfather," he said more carefully. "When my sister went to bed last night, she was healthy and happy and almost cured of a small illness I had been treating. But this morning she woke up so sick that I fear for her life. Fighting Bear slept with us last night and had a dream that our house was burning and that I was the only one outside to fight the fire. When he woke up this morning his leg hurt so much he couldn't stand on it. Well, he is sure that his dream was a warning that only *I* will be able to cure Red-bird." Soaring Hawk paused then continued cautiously,

"But I don't think I can go out all alone. I thought perhaps that if I took an assistant, one who really knew things, then it would be better. But I would have to be the one in charge."

Soaring Hawk glanced at Owl to see if he should proceed. The look he saw on the old man's face shattered his courage. Abruptly he rose to his feet. There seemed to be no sense in going further.

"Thank you for your time so early in the morning, Grandfather. I must be going now. Our homestead is always open to you."

"Sit down," Owl commanded. "Is that any way for a medicine man to act? How can you expect to cure your sister if you do not follow your heart? What has your uncle been doing if he has not taught you this? Your heart sent you here to seek my help. Do you not even have the courage to ask for it?"

"Actually it was my mother who first suggested I come."

"Yes, Easy Dancer has always been a wise woman. Perhaps she gave you the idea, and it is your heart that told you it was a good idea, and it is your heart that has brought you here. Now perhaps you would like to finish your business before you leave."

Soaring Hawk sat down again. "Grandfather," he said, "you are a powerful and wise beloved old man, and I would not even be worthy to be your own assistant. Yet I am asking you to come be mine so that I can save my sister's life."

Owl paused thoughtfully. Then he said, "Shouldn't you tell me whom I would be helping you conjure against?"

"I can't tell you that unless you agree to help," said Soaring Hawk.

"Well, how can I know that you aren't going against someone from my own clan?"

"I'm not after a Paint."

Owl nodded approvingly. "You are right to tell me no more. Misplaced trust can bring defeat to even the most powerful medicine man." Owl fell silent and stared into the fire. His eyes shone and the thousand wrinkles on his face seemed to have shifted upward. The old man looked happy.

"I knew when I got up this morning that it was going to be an unusual day," said Owl. "I am going to go with you to fight Scratcher."

Soaring Hawk stiffened. How did he know it was Scratcher?

"Who else could it be?" said Owl. "Everyone will think of Scratcher first."

"It's true," admitted Soaring Hawk, relaxing. "Everyone knows about the feud. Scratcher has not tried at all to hide his red heart. Surely he must know he'll be the first to be suspected. I wonder what he thinks he is doing."

"That is for you to find out," said Owl.

"Yes, and I will," Soaring Hawk said confidently. "I'll leave now so I can do what has to be done before we go conjure tonight. Fever and having pains in different places are the things I will give her medicine for. Maybe that will keep her from getting worse while I'm working against Scratcher. And then there's the business of night-goers. The protection we put on four nights ago has run out now, so I'll have to see that it gets done tonight to last for four more nights."

"How are you going to do that at your house at sundown and be at the river at the same time?" asked Owl.

"I'm not sure yet. I was thinking of having everything done ahead of time and leaving Fighting Bear to walk around the house and say the words, but I'm afraid his leg won't let him. I'll have to think of some other way."

Owl used two small sticks to take a coal from the fire to light his pipe. Then he sat quietly, blowing smoke rings. Soaring Hawk moved to leave, but Owl began to speak.

"Your mother has always been a wise woman," the

old man said. "When she was younger than you I almost took her on as my apprentice. But then Wren's Nest took on Fighting Bear, and I had to drop the idea. There was too much risk in teaching what I knew to the sister of my rival's apprentice." Owl shook his head sadly. "I never found anyone else I wanted to teach."

Soaring Hawk looked at him curiously. He had never heard that about his mother. "Do you think I could tell her the words? If she could walk around the house for me, that problem would be solved."

"She could do it."

Soaring Hawk rose. "Then that is what I will do. I have to be going on now. I wish I could say I have to be getting home for breakfast, but of course I'll be fasting all day. That won't be necessary for you, though."

"You are very kind to a feeble old man, Grandchild. But the more purity we keep, the more power you will have. When you are as old as I am, you will know that it is almost easier to fast than it is to eat."

"However you want it then. I'll meet you when the sun is half down toward the west. I'll be at the place where the red oak leans over the water."

As Soaring Hawk ducked out the door, he had a thought. He would have let it go if Owl had not noticed his hesitation and said, "What is it, Grandchild?"

"I was just thinking," said Soaring Hawk. "If we had an ulunsuti crystal I know we could beat Scratcher."

"That certainly would make it easier," Owl said with a smile. "Do you have one?"

Soaring Hawk had to grin at the thought of it. "No, of course not. But I have a chickadee skin and an otter pouch and a beautiful bear pipe. What more do we need?"

He waved goodbye and left the old man sitting alone.

"What more indeed," said Owl as he lit up his pipe again.

Eight

Soaring Hawk stood over Redbird's bed and gazed down with great feeling at the only sister he had in the world. She lay still, almost deathlike. He spoke her name and her eyes opened, but they stared past him, vacant and unseeing. He turned away from her and headed out the door. Chestnut Bread looked up from tending the outside fire and watched him as he came across the yard. He stopped beside her and for a moment they stood together in silence.

"She'll be all right," said Chestnut Bread.

"She will," Soaring Hawk said softly. He turned then and left the homestead.

The sun hung low in the Darkening Land as Soaring Hawk and Owl went quietly along the river trail. Old Owl had kept him waiting at their meeting place, and Soaring Hawk had been afraid that there would not be time to get to the place he had in mind for the ceremony before sunset. But now he saw how swiftly the old man could move, and he was no longer worried.

They could have taken a shorter path, one that left the river and ran more directly to Soaring Hawk's special place far up in the mountains. But he wanted to stay within the sound of the river's song and feel its power and let it gather and build inside him. Power was now the guiding force by which he calculated everything. He was painted with power, red for war. Black Fox had helped him paint the intricate and fiercely beautiful designs that covered his body. He wore only a breechcloth and carried nothing with him but his medicine things in the otter pouch and some hot coals in a little clay pot that hung in a leather sling from his shoulder. He carried no food. It was a gesture of his confidence in overcoming Scratcher in one night. Tomorrow he would be back home eating stew and corn bread and smiling proudly at Redbird, who would be well on her way to recovery.

Suddenly his stomach growled, and he sucked in his belly to stifle the sound. It felt good to be hungry. It felt powerful.

Twice they stopped so that Owl could rest. The old man did not ask to stop, but neither did he complain when they did. Old is old, thought Soaring Hawk, no matter how young the man seemed or how powerful. Old Owl did indeed look powerful. He wore an old feather cape made of white egret feathers. Obviously left over from his days as head medicine man, it was ragged and soiled, with more than a few gaps where some of the feathers had fallen out, but beautiful just the same. His headdress of swan feathers was in somewhat better condition. The feathers had yellowed, but they were all there standing proudly in a crown about his head. Soaring Hawk was pleased that Owl had dressed so finely for the occasion and that he had even taken pains to paint himself from head to toe with beautiful white designs. Surely Scratcher did not suspect what power he was facing—a young red man ready to fight fiercely to victory in the battle of conjury and beside him an old beloved white man like the river, an ever-flowing source of wisdom and power.

When they reached their destination, Owl nodded approvingly. "It is a good place," he said. From the Sun Land in the east the shimmering river rushed headlong down the mountain, colliding with boulders and tumbling over a low rocky shelf into a small, clear pool as deep as a man's waist. The mountain forest towered overhead, while on the banks, scattered among the ferns and wild flowers, lichen-covered boulders lay still and quiet upon the damp earth like so many great turtles offering their backs as seats to whoever might happen by, whether man or beast or spirit. It was a beautiful place, and Soaring Hawk could feel its power.

There was power too in the little fire he built. It was kindled from coals of Ancient Fire that he had brought from the town. Ancient Fire smoldered in the depths of the townhouse mound, where it never died and never became unclean. The head medicine man knew how to bring it up from its resting place, and each year during the New Corn Festival he used it to re-light the townhouse fire, and this in turn was used to relight the fires in all the households of the town. Any-one could make ordinary fire, and it worked as well as Ancient Fire for many things, but only Ancient Fire could help move the forces of the world.

Soaring Hawk began to take things from his medi-cine bag. On the bank close to the water he spread a piece of black skin and placed on it four black beads—black for the Darkening Land; black for doom; black for death; and black for Scratcher, whose curse would soon be turned back upon his own evil head. Beside this he spread a red skin and placed four red beads upon it—red for the Sun Land; red for victory; red for the power to overcome the most hateful of ene-mies; and red for Redbird and the victorious Deer people.

"Scratcher is crazy to go against us. He'll never be stronger than the Deer people are," said Soaring Hawk. He was trying now to weaken Scratcher's power by deriding him.

"It is stupid for him to try," said Owl. "A man should know his limitations. Scratcher is good for noth-ing more than curing the aching joints of old people. He is a weak and despicable worm."

"He's so stupid he thinks he's smart. He thinks he can beat the Deer people by going against me instead of Fighting Bear. What an idiot! What does he think Fighting Bear has been doing all these years? Teaching me to sew beads? I know everything Fighting Bear knows. It's going to be easy to beat a stupid toad like Scratcher."

"Do you know what he makes me think of?" asked Owl.

"What?"

"A possum. A stupid possum. Do you know why?"

"Why?" grinned Soaring Hawk.

"Because a possum shuffles along through the dry leaves making the most racket you've ever heard, and a bobcat can find him as easy as he can find the sun on a cloudless day. So what does the possum do? Well, if he has time, he climbs a tree. But the bobcat can climb trees too. So what does the possum do now? Does he fight? No, because he has no power against this enemy of his. All that possum can do is go dead with fear. Just like Scratcher. He is probably climbing a tree right now."

Soaring Hawk chuckled, but in his stomach anxiety clutched at him. This brave talk was well enough, but it was not going to win the battle. He was going to have to do that himself by calling stronger forces to his side than Scratcher could call to his.

The sun was setting. It was time to start. As he took his gourd rattle from his pouch and a bead from each skin and waded with Owl a little way into the water, he could feel his confidence sliding away. Was it because Scratcher was off somewhere talking down his power? If he was, he was doing a good job of it.

"You take the beads," said Soaring Hawk, handing them to Owl. "I'll do everything else. I'll say all the words and you'll just be holding the beads for me, nothing more."

That seemed to satisfy Owl, who now stood solemnly with the cold water rushing about his legs. His arms were extended before him toward the growing darkness of the Sun Land, and he held a bead gingerly between the thumb and forefinger of each of his old gnarled hands. Soaring Hawk fixed his eyes on the red

bead in Owl's right hand. If his song was powerful
enough to bring victory, the red bead would move in
Owl's fingers while the black bead stayed still. He
stood quietly for a moment and then began to shake
his gourd rattle, and a chant rose softly from his lips:

"Hey, Red Bead! Listen while I call you.
Now you are coming down to us, you who never
  fail in anything.
Like a red blanket your power is covering her.
Now she is no longer blue.
She is sitting and asking for food.
Now the fever has been taken away.
Relief has come.

"Hey, Red Bead! Listen while I call you.
Now you are coming down to us, you who never
  fail in anything.
Like the red morning sun breaking
  over the mountains
Your power is covering her.
Now she is standing and laughing with her
  friends.
Relief has come.

"Hey, Red Bead! Listen while I call you.
Now you are coming down to us, you who never
  fail in anything.
Like the red warmth of the fire in the winter
  house
Your power is covering him.
Now he is standing without pain.
Only a stick is needed to steady his steps.
Relief has come.

"Hey, Red Bead! Listen while I call you.
Now you are coming down to us, you who never
  fail in anything.
Like the smoke from the red pipes of many warriors

Your power is covering me.
Like a lowly worm my enemy quakes at the
    thought of me.
Now I can brush him away like a mere ant.
Now my soul is being lifted to the highest place of
    power
And my lineage will live forever.
Relief has come."

As Soaring Hawk sang, he watched the beads. Red-bird's bead, the red one, had been the first to move. It had shifted around ever so slightly between Owl's thumb and forefinger, and then it began to wiggle, moving at first around the tip of his finger and then working its way down to the first joint. Then the black bead, Scratcher's bead, also began to move, but it was staying on Owl's fingertip as if it had no strength to do anything more. Soaring Hawk was pleased, even surprised, at the remarkable ease of his victory.

But all at once Scratcher's bead came alive. With strong, powerful movements it wriggled down past the first joint almost to the bottom of Owl's finger, and then as if it were laughing at the red bead, it climbed back up to the tip and then snaked its way back down. The red bead seemed petrified at the other's performance, and it retreated to Owl's fingertip, where it stayed for the rest of the song, rocking back and forth and showing no strong movements whatsoever.

Soaring Hawk was horrified, but in his hand the rattle kept on, never hesitating, never missing a beat. He was not beaten yet. He would not let his sister die. He had another song to sing. He opened each of his senses to the world and tried to draw more power to himself. He looked all around—at the sky where red streaks were fading into darkness, at the great trees with leaves black against the sky, at the water rushing over its bed, at the little fire glowing ever more brightly in the gathering darkness. He listened—to the gourd rattle, to the water, to the night sounds coming to life

in the forest. He felt the cold water on his legs and the
warm breeze on his face. And he thought about the
words of the song to be sung and drew them into himself and mixed them with the gathering darkness and
the smoke of the fire and the cold water on his legs
and the damp moss and the leaves black against the
sky until the song burst forth from his lips with a surge
of power such as he had never felt before:

"Hey, Black Bead! Listen while I call you.
Now you are coming down to us, you who never
    fail in anything.
Like the black cloud that rolls in with a thunder-
    storm
Your power is covering him.
Now his power is falling away from him
And the things he knows are no good to him.
His power has become nothing.

"Hey, Black Bead! Listen while I call you.
Now you are coming down to us, you who never
    fail in anything.
Like the darkness of a black, moonless night
Your power is covering him.
Now his wives despise him, and they are looking
    to be unfaithful.
Now his corn is eaten by worms
And his squash is rotting on the vine.
His power has become nothing.

"Hey Black Bead! Listen while I call you.
Now you are coming down to us, you who never
    fail in anything.
Like the terrible black water at the depth
    of a great whirlpool
Your power is covering him.
Now his dogs are sick and dying.
Now the dwellers of the woods hear him coming
    and hide from him.

Now his hunting songs are no good to him.
His power has become nothing.

"Hey, Black Bead! Listen while I call you.
Now you are coming down to us, you who never
    fail in anything.
Like the horrible black breath of a great uktena
Your power is covering him.
Now his soul is slipping from him.
Now it has been carried to the Darkening Land
And buried in the black mud and covered with a
    black rock.
Now it is lost in the Darkening Land
And it will never return.
His name is Scratcher of the Wolf clan.
His power has become nothing."

But it was no good. He knew at once that it was no good. He had watched the beads. Scratcher's black one had never slowed, and the red one, the one that was Redbird's life, had never moved again from Owl's fingertip. Tears of anguish welled up in his eyes as he brought the ceremony to an end by plunging himself four times beneath the water of the little pool. That was the best song he had ever sung, and still it had not been enough to overcome Scratcher.

But the cool waters of the mountain stream were soothing, and by the time he came out of the water some of his despair had washed away. Dripping wet, his body paint smeared and running, he sat down heavily on a rock near Owl.

"I guess Scratcher was ready for us," he said.

"I guess so," said Owl. The old man's arms were trembling from having been held out in front of him for so long.

"But I guess this is about what we expected for the first try."

"That's about right," said Owl. "And so if you think

about it, that means that everything is going as we planned."

Soaring Hawk looked up and caught the twinkle in the old man's eye. "But Grandfather, that last song was the best I've ever done, and it hardly even slowed him down."

"It didn't slow him down at all as far as I could see," chuckled Owl. "But a good medicine man is never finished. My best song will be the last one I sing before I die."

Soaring Hawk added another stick of wood to the fire. Owl was right. Redbird was not going to die this instant. There was time. He could wait until midnight and have four more tries at Scratcher before dawn. If he was still unsuccessful, he could wait and have a second night to try, and then a third night, and even a fourth night, if need be. Of course, he would only be able to eat once a day, just before sundown, and he would not be able to sleep at all, day or night, until the whole affair was finished. In this contest of one man's power against another's, if either man slept, even for a moment, the power that he had gathered since the ordeal began would rush from him like partridges scared up in a meadow. The enemy would step in to take the advantage, and in an instant the battle would be over.

"Do you think we need to build a shelter for only one night?" asked Owl.

Soaring Hawk tried to sound confident. "Why bother? We'll be going home tomorrow. Home to venison stew."

"And corn dumplings."

"And hominy," grinned Soaring Hawk.

"And mountain onions," chuckled Owl.

"And bean bread, if only we had some beans left."

"And roasting ears, if only it were after the festival."

Night had gathered around them, and in the flickering light of the small campfire the two conjurers laughed together and rubbed their stomachs hungrily.

If their empty bellies were any proof of their power, then their power at that moment was mighty indeed.

Laughter was refreshing; it brought a measure of peace. They sat quietly for a while staring into the fire and listening to the tumbling waters of the stream. Soaring Hawk's thoughts wandered back over the events of the day, and after a while he said, "I hope I didn't do something stupid today."

"What did you do?"

"I asked Chestnut Bread to stay at our homestead and help my mother."

"Why did you do that?"

"My mother needed the help, and Chestnut Bread offered."

"Why would she offer to work against her father?"

"Nobody told her we thought it was Scratcher."

"You didn't think she could figure it out like everybody else?"

"Perhaps if she wanted to," said Soaring Hawk. "But I don't think she is with Scratcher in this feud. After all, she is not a Wolf, you know. She's a Paint."

"You don't have to tell a Paint who else is a Paint," said Owl. "I know she's a Paint. I know she's a fine person. But what makes you think she would take sides against her father?"

"Redbird has always been her best friend, ever since they were small. I don't think Chestnut Bread would betray someone who in her heart is the same as a sister to her. But that's not the only reason I trust her. There are things she has told me that make me think she's not on Scratcher's side. There was a story she told me about one of her fathers. It makes him look awfully foolish. Why would she tell me that if she were on the side of the Wolf people?"

"I'd like to hear that story," grinned Owl.

"I swore not to tell."

"Okay. But tell me this. What did your uncle think of her staying to help?"

"He was against it. I could see it in his face. But he

didn't say anything. I almost changed my mind, but I knew my mother needed the help."

"And now you are uncertain again," said Owl. "Maybe someone has his eye on a certain girl and is afraid his passions have clouded his judgment."

Soaring Hawk looked away in embarrassment.

"Well, I don't think you should worry too much about it," said Owl. "If all that you say is true, then I would say your judgment was sound. Perhaps I would have done the same."

"But I'm never really sure what she means when she says things," said Soaring Hawk. "That's the trouble with her."

"Then all we can do is hope for the best. It is too late to do anything else."

Between midnight and dawn Soaring Hawk conjured four more times against Scratcher, but each attempt met with failure. Now, in the soft light of foggy dawn he worked with Owl to throw up a rough lean-to. They would be there through another night, and they might as well be comfortable. In truth, Soaring Hawk cared nothing for comfort. He was building the lean-to because it was something to do. It gave him moments of forgetfulness, moments when he did not see Redbird lying deathlike on her bed, staring past him with vacant eyes. But only moments. The other, the reality, kept rushing back.

"I think he really is trying to kill her," he said.

"What did you think he was trying to do?" asked Owl.

"I don't know. Not kill her. Not over something as small as the rain dispute."

"Then you think he should have given up by now? Why should he? If he does, the curse will come back on his own head. He would be crazy to do that."

"That would be nothing. Just as soon as I turned it back on him, he could send it down the river to another town. That's how I was hoping this thing was going to end. Now I don't think so."

Owl was lashing poles together and made no reply.

"Why would he choose Redbird?" asked Soaring Hawk. "Why not me? Or my mother? Or Fighting Bear himself? Why is he trying to kill my sister? My only sister?"

"Don't you know?" Owl asked, without looking up.

"Yes. I know," said Soaring Hawk, and a great sadness came over him. "My mother cannot bear children any longer. If my sister dies now, our lineage dies with her. I'll finish out my life alone with no nieces or nephews, no sister to care for, no family to go home to when I need a rest. . . . I never thought I would have to face such misery. Maybe I'll give up medicine and become a warrior and go on all the most dangerous missions until I find an early death. I'll earn glory for my people and save myself the agony of growing old without kinsmen."

"So you've given up already."

"No! I haven't. It's just that I can't get used to what is happening. I keep thinking of her dying. . . . But I haven't given up."

"That's good, because there is still a lot you can do. You have to build up your power, Grandchild, and power is more than fasting and paint and songs. Power is knowledge, and knowledge is everywhere. It is in fire and in water. It is in the sun and moon and stars. It is in the wind, and in the mountains. Knowledge is in the stories you've heard in the square. It is all around you, waiting to be seen and heard and felt. And knowledge is even buried deep inside your own heart, waiting for you to understand its meaning. This is a great trial that has come to you, but it is one that a good man can pass through in glory."

Soaring Hawk leaned against the frame of the lean-to and closed his eyes. He was tired and sleepy, he was hungry, and he was overwhelmed by the greatness of his plight. He felt himself in darkness, lost in the middle of some great and silent void. Then a sound began to grow in his awareness, a sound that moved toward him, reaching for him in the darkness of his despair. It was water tumbling over rocks, swirling in eddies, rushing headlong down the mountainside. The sound became everything until it was as if the river were washing over him, and he heard Long Man talking to him, telling him things of great importance, things that he needed to know. . . . But the words were in another language, and Soaring Hawk did not know them.

"Grandfather," he murmured, not opening his eyes. "Can you hear what the river is saying?"

"No, Grandchild," Owl said softly. "It isn't talking to me."

Nine

Dawn was cheerless at the Deer homestead. Chestnut Bread awoke with the first morning light and took Easy Dancer's place beside Redbird's bed while Easy Dancer went wearily into the other room of the house to try to get some sleep. Fighting Bear too had been awake all night, but he remained seated by the hearth, silent and grim, making no move to retire. In his eyes he was somewhere else. Black Fox had been up and down throughout the night and now he was preparing to leave the house to go down to the river, where he would plunge into the water and sing songs to the forces of the world. It was the usual thing for him to do at dawn, but Chestnut Bread knew that on this morning he would be there a very long time—he would be singing songs for Redbird. Black Fox fastened back the door mat as he left, letting golden light filter in to lift the shadows from the room. But the light did not lift the blue shadow from Chestnut Bread's heart as she sat watching over her friend. And it did not help her decide what to do.

It was a question of whether to go home and remain at home, or go home and then return. Either way, she had to go home. Last evening she had sent her younger brother with a message to her mothers telling them she was staying the night at the Deer homestead. Today they would expect her to bring her own message. She knew what she wanted to tell them, and in her mind she imagined the encounter she would have with Corn Tassel, her own stout mother.

"I just came home to get some things, Mother. I'm going back and help Easy Dancer until Redbird is well."

"Oh, is that so? And what about your father?"

"My gentle father? He's not involved in this."

"You know which father I mean."

"My tall father? Why should I care about him? You should see what he's doing to Redbird! He's wrong, Mother! He's evil! I hate him now! I don't have to respect him anymore! My gentle father should disown him. The whole Wolf clan should disown him."

"You talk like someone who has lost her senses. My husband would never forsake his brother and you should never forsake your fathers. Sit down and calm yourself, Daughter. Tell me about Redbird. How is she this morning?"

"Do you think I am so foolish that I would tell you that? You're on their side. You'll tell my gentle father and he'll tell his brother. They want you to ask me things about her, but I won't tell you. I'm leaving. I'm going back there to stay."

Chestnut Bread sighed. What an utter calamity it would be to defy her mothers and take sides against her fathers. She would never be able to go home again. Every person in the town would know about it and hate her for it. She would have to leave, and where in the world could she go? It was impossible. She would have to go home today and stay home. Someone else would help Easy Dancer. Even if she were to stay here, others were sure to come. Relatives of Black Fox, friends, neighbors. They would come today or tomorrow, whenever they heard how bad things were. In the long run it would not really matter to Redbird and Easy Dancer whether she stayed away or not. But what about Soaring Hawk? What would he think if she abandoned them now, before anyone else had come to help? She knew the answer. He would scorn her for betraying his trust, and in her heart she knew she could never bear his scorn.

Chestnut Bread looked at Redbird. Her breathing was strong enough. If only she would move. It was frightening to see her lying so still. The sun rose over the mountains and the light grew brighter inside the summer house. Then suddenly Redbird stirred. Chestnut Bread's heart leaped and she leaned close to her friend, speaking her name. Briefly Redbird opened her eyes. When she closed them again it was as if she were retreating behind some barricade, and Chestnut Bread, though she tried, could not reach her or call her back. Sadly she abandoned her effort, and through the long morning she watched and waited in misery and uncertainty.

At last Black Fox came back. At the hearth he dropped a load of sourwood to be used against night-goers. And then he came over to his daughter where she lay quiet and still, and stroked her hair sadly.

"I'll sit with her now," he said to Chestnut Bread. "You've been good to stay with us, but your mothers must be wondering about you."

"I suppose they are," said Chestnut Bread. She wondered if she were being asked to leave and not return. "Perhaps they will let me come back."

"Perhaps," said Black Fox. "My son has made it clear that you are welcome in this homestead."

"And you in ours," Chestnut Bread said softly as she rose. She turned and bid polite farewell to Fighting Bear, but he did not look up or take any notice of her leaving.

She came to her own homestead in the sweltering heat of midday. Here were people of all ages, from beloved old people to tiny babies, and children—so many children running about laughing and shouting, all brothers and sisters, children of the same lineage. What a difference between this place and the sad, quiet little homestead she had just left. Here the buildings were so many that there was not even room for all of them around one yard, and a second yard was gradually being enclosed. If Easy Dancer's lineage had a homestead like this one, there would be no reason for Chestnut Bread to go back. There would be no need for any outside help at all.

Chestnut Bread walked slowly through the yard, dreading the encounter with her mother. For everyone but the children it was the quiet part of the day. Even the dogs had retreated to their favorite shady places. Beneath the eaves of one of the summer houses Chestnut Bread's mothers' uncle sat snoring. He was the oldest person in the homestead, and no matter what was going on around him, he was always dozing off to sleep. In the doorway of another summer house Chestnut Bread's beloved old grandmother sat weaving baskets with one of her daughters, Chestnut Bread's laughing mother. The two women talked quietly together as their busy fingers flew about their work, and the basket designs seemed to bloom almost unnoticed. Chestnut Bread found her stout mother, her true mother, sitting alone under the shady hickory tree coiling pottery. She stood quietly, and after a time her mother spoke.

"You've come home," said Corn Tassel. "How is Redbird today?"

"She is resting," said Chestnut Bread, taking care to reveal nothing that would help Scratcher in any way. She watched her mother's quick, experienced hands work the clay.

Corn Tassel was silent for a while. She rolled a lump of clay into a ropelike piece and coiled it around the edge of a half-finished bowl, building up the sides.

"My father was a member of the Deer clan," she said without looking up from her work. "He came from the village of Swan Place." Chestnut Bread stood unmoved. She had heard about her grandfather before, a hundred times it seemed. "He met your grandmother while she was visiting some of her father's people there. After a while they wanted to marry, but there was the problem of going to a wife so far from home. Finally his uncles decided that since he had three older brothers who could take care of his two sisters, it would be all right for him to go away to marry. And so he came from that town to this one. I remember my father as a jolly man who was always making us laugh, but your grandmother tells me that sometimes he would get lonely for home. He would want to be with Deer people again. At those times he would visit Redbird's grandmother and her children, Easy Dancer and Fighting Bear. They were the only clansmen he had in this town, and they were always kind to him and cheered him up. When I was very young, maybe nine years old, he took me with him to Swan Place to visit his people. They were good people, Daughter. They gave me one of the happiest times of my life. But soon after our trip to Swan Place, my father died and made that long journey to the Darkening Land. It seems now that it was a long time ago, but in all the days that have passed I have never forgotten my father, and still today I would never want to see harm come to the Deer people, no matter who might try to bring it to them."

Tears welled up in Chestnut Bread's eyes. Often she had heard the story, but never had it meant so much as now. She sat down in misery beside her mother and opened her heart.

"What am I to do?" she asked. "Redbird is worse today. Soaring Hawk left yesterday to conjure for her, but today she's worse than before he went. Who but my tall father could be doing it? I try to think of who else could be doing it, but who else, who in the whole town, would want to?"

"That's what everyone would like to know. Your gentle father has gone looking for Scratcher to find out for himself what is going on."

"And what if he comes back and tells us that Scratcher *is* the one? Then what am I supposed to do? Go against my own father's people? Take the other side against them? All the town would turn against me. 'She went against her father,' they would say. It wouldn't matter if *they* were against Scratcher, too—he isn't their father, so they can take whatever side they want."

"It is the way things are," said Corn Tassel. "We don't belong to our father's people, but still we owe them great respect. Nothing can change that."

"But what about Redbird and all the years we've been like sisters? Who's going to help her mother cook food, and carry water, and fix medicine, and do everything that has to be done at times like this? And Soaring Hawk! He trusted me for the color of my heart and asked me to stay to help him save his lineage. He thinks I'm there now instead of back at my own homestead wondering whether or not I'll even go back again. He gave me all his trust, but look at me now."

"So that's what confuses your heart," said Corn Tassel. "Soaring Hawk has taken it and spun it around."

Chestnut Bread's face streamed with tears and she rocked gently back and forth with quiet sobs. But her anguish did not spring from her uncertainty, for suddenly she knew what she would do. Scratcher had all of the Wolf clan to stand beside him, but Soaring Hawk had no one. She could see herself doing nothing else but going back to the Deer people, even though she knew what it would mean. Everyone would know about it and scorn her for it. She would no longer be welcome in Wolf homesteads, and if she were ever allowed back in her mothers' homestead, it would only be with her own father's scorn. There was no way of knowing how long it would be before people forgot about it altogether. Perhaps they never would. So she would go to Soaring Hawk if he would have her and make her home with the Deer people. Maybe for her sake they would move to another town.

"I'll disgrace our lineage," she whispered sadly.

"My daughter is a fighter," said Corn Tassel, "but it

is hard to fight the ways of our people. Perhaps you don't have to yet."

Chestnut Bread looked up.

"Do you know who's conjuring against the Deer people?" Corn Tassel asked.

Chestnut Bread gave her a puzzled look. "It's like we said. It must be Scratcher."

"But do you know that for a fact?"

Suddenly Chestnut Bread understood what her mother was saying. She wiped her tears and a little smile began to grow. "No. I don't know it for a fact. No one has said a word to me about it. You only said that my gentle father has gone to find out what's going on."

"Then I think you had better leave quickly before he comes back and tells you."

Chestnut Bread jumped to her feet. It was the most promising thing she had heard all day. Maybe it was just a trick in thinking. Maybe no one would accept it when it was all over, but for now she could at least leave the homestead with her stout mother's blessing. "I don't know when I'll be back," she said. "I'll stay till Soaring Hawk gets home."

"He's not a very good hunter, you know."

Chestnut Bread smiled broadly. "He would hate to hear you say that. Anyway, I'm not worried about it. He was always a good hunter before, and I know he'll be good again. Everyone has bad luck now and then."

"I hope a little bad luck is all it is," said Corn Tassel. "If you don't get a hunter when you get a husband, I'm afraid you don't get very much at all."

Chestnut Bread left and went straight to the Deer homestead. When she reached the edge of the yard, she stopped. Would they really want her back, or would they think she was a spy? She saw Fighting Bear sitting outside by the fire. He was the one who seemed to distrust her the most. She could understand it, though. He didn't know her as well as the others did.

Then she saw Easy Dancer come out and wave to her, and she knew that she was welcome.

"I'm glad you came back, Little Daughter," said Easy Dancer. "I need to go for water at the river."

"I'll go for you," said Chestnut Bread.

"It would be nice for you to sit with Redbird," said Easy Dancer. "My husband thinks I should get out and move around."

"I'll sit with her then. I'll be glad to." She followed Easy Dancer back into the summer house.

"My husband has gone to the square," said Easy Dancer. "If you need help for anything, call Fighting Bear. Otherwise perhaps you can keep from disturbing him. I'm hoping he'll get some sleep."

"He seems tired."

"And he's very worried, I'm afraid." Easy Dancer's face twisted with emotion as she picked up two water jars and hurried out the door.

Chestnut Bread stood by Redbird's bed and gazed down at her ashen face. Was she dying? Chestnut Bread had seen people die. She knew the different ways it happened. There was old Shoe-Boots, her grandmother's oldest brother. He had been delirious before he died. He raved on and on about turtles in trees. He said he saw old friends and relatives standing about the room, people who had been gone for years. And in the middle of one of his tirades he simply expired.

But with Cornflower, Chestnut Bread's little niece, it had been different. It still pained her heart to think of it. They could not keep the child in bed. She sat on the floor and played as if nothing was wrong, and all the while her little body was burning up with fever. Only on the last day did she lie quietly and cry a little. That was the way Cornflower died.

And then there was Smoker, one of Chestnut Bread's clan brothers. He died from a leg wound that wouldn't heal. In his last days he grew weaker and weaker, and he slept a lot, but when he was awake he was very much himself, carrying on coherent conversations to the end. Chestnut Bread had seen all these people die, but never had she seen any sick person, dying or not, lie there as listlessly as Redbird, so completely separated from the world around her. She had heard of people who had been like this, though, and she knew the seriousness of it. She looked at Redbird for a long time, and then she decided to try to rouse her.

"Could you drink some water?" she asked. It was like asking a dead person, but Chestnut Bread got a dipper of water and lifted Redbird's head and held the water to her lips. To her surprise, Redbird opened her eyes and drank a little. Chestnut Bread lowered her head again and set the water aside. She saw the emptiness in Redbird's eyes, how they stared ahead without seeing. Chestnut Bread leaned close. "What are you thinking about, Little Sister? It's me. It's Chestnut Bread. Talk to me and tell me what you're thinking about." She tried to entice with her voice. She wanted to penetrate the dreadful wall, to reach in and grab Redbird before it was too late. But Redbird's eyes remained vacant, her face ashen and lifeless. It was no good. There was nothing anyone could do. With great sadness, Chestnut Bread sat back and began to prepare her heart for sorrow and grief.

"Different things," a strange voice said suddenly, and Chestnut Bread leaped to her feet. She peered out the door, but saw only Fighting Bear nodding by the fire. The she realized who had spoken. She looked around at Redbird and smiled to see that her gaze was met. Redbird's voice had sounded odd and distant, but at least she had spoken.

"What kinds of things?" Chestnut Bread asked tenderly, moving quickly to the bedside.

"My lineage," Redbird whispered. "It goes with me."

"Where are you going, Little Sister?"

"To the Darkening Land. Grandmother's there."

"But you'll leave Soaring Hawk all alone."

"I don't want to go," said Redbird, and a tear slipped away as she closed her eyes again. Chestnut Bread leaned closer.

"You don't have to go, Little Sister. You must fight to stay. Soaring Hawk can cure you if you let him have the time he needs. He has three more nights, and that's how long you have to fight. Then if nothing happens, you can let go. Then you can go to your grandmother. But first you have to fight."

Redbird opened her eyes and slowly brought her gaze to rest on the face of her friend. "Yes," she murmured. "But you must give me something to hold on to." Her voice trailed off and she gave a little sigh.

"Rest now, Little Sister," said Chestnut Bread. "You need to rest for the fight. But when I call you again, you must reach out to me. Will you come back again when I call you?"

Redbird nodded.

Chestnut Bread sat back with new hope and watched her as she slept. After a little while had passed, she heard activity in the yard. Then there were voices. Fighting Bear's came first:

"Did you learn anything?"

"Scratcher has gone from the town." That was the voice of Black Fox, who had evidently just arrived from the square. Chestnut Bread got up silently and moved to the door to listen. "He told his wives he was going out to hunt," said Black Fox. "But listen to the way he said it: 'I don't know when I'll be back,' he told them, 'I'm going deer hunting.' *Deer* hunting! Now what do you think of that?" Black Fox's voice suddenly loomed close and Chestnut Bread dashed back to her seat. He came in and went to Redbird's bed, where he stood staring at her for a long time. Then he turned and looked strangely at Chestnut Bread. She braced herself. She would hardly blame him for throwing her out—after all, Scratcher *was* one of her fathers.

"Are you strong enough to help watch for night-goers?" said Black Fox. "My wife may need you tonight. She's wearing down."

"I've watched before," said Chestnut Bread. "When my niece was sick."

"Alone?"

"No. Not alone."

"It's more frightening to watch alone," said Black Fox, and then he left the room.

When she was awakened that night, Chestnut Bread at first thought that it was morning and that it was Corn Tassel who was shaking her gently by the shoulder. But when she saw Easy Dancer's face, she remembered everything, and as she sat up anxiety tugged at her heart.

"You were sleeping so soundly, I hated to wake you," said Easy Dancer. "But I was afraid I could not stay awake much longer. You won't have to watch long. It's almost dawn."

"You should have gotten me up sooner," said Chestnut Bread. She went to a water jar by the door and rubbed cold water on her face to chase away the sleep. "You must be awfully tired."

"Not as tired as my son must be, Little Daughter. This is a time for extra strength from the Deer people. For us everything is at stake. We cannot ask our Paint friend to share equally in our troubles."

"I wouldn't mind."

Easy Dancer smiled gratefully. "I'll be right here if you need me. Wake me up if you become frightened. And don't forget that the men are out there." She nodded toward the door. "They're watching too."

"I'll be all right," said Chestnut Bread.

Easy Dancer lay down on the bed that Chestnut Bread had used, a bed against the wall, not far from Redbird. In no time at all Chestnut Bread heard in her breathing that she was asleep, and she felt at once the loneliness of her vigil. She reminded herself that Black Fox and Fighting Bear were in the yard by the fire and that at least one of them would be awake and watching. There was comfort in that: It would be hard to watch if one were all alone.

Because night-goers could disguise themselves or even become invisible, watching for them was not a simple thing. But there was a way to do it. If you made a small mound of hot ashes from Ancient Fire and sprinkled it with tobacco, the tobacco would spark whenever a night-goer came near. On whichever side of the ashes the spark appeared, that was the side of the house where the night-goer was. If the night-goer had made himself invisible and had gotten inside the room, the tobacco would make a brilliant flash and the night-goer would fall dead, or maybe creep away to die.

The ashes Easy Dancer had been using had grown cold, and Chestnut Bread scraped them back into the fire. She pulled out some new ones and made them into a neat little pile on a hearthstone. From a small clay bowl she took a pinch of powdered tobacco and sprinkled it over the ashes. On the back side of the ashes a little spark appeared and was gone. She added a stick of sourwood to the fire.

Knowing that there was a night-goer out somewhere behind the house was not too terribly frightening. The ring of tobacco smoke that Easy Dancer had put around the house yesterday evening would last for four nights, and it would serve as an effective barrier against all but the most powerful night-goers. It was the powerful ones who were so frightening. If one of them took a notion to steal Redbird's liver, it could come marching right in through tobacco smoke, sourwood smoke, and everything else they could think of to throw up against it. The only way to fight a night-goer like that was to recognize its true identity and call it by name. Then it would change back to its real self, and he or she would go home and lie down and wait for the death that would come without fail in four days. But it was extremely difficult to recognize a night-goer. To do that you had to fast for four days and nights and drink a brew made from the root of a certain plant—Chestnut Bread was not sure which one. And then, *maybe* you could have the power that you needed. Fighting Bear had that power, she reminded herself. He was out there right now watching with his own pile of ashes. If night-goers got too close he would come inside where Redbird was, and no night-goer would dare follow him in.

Chestnut Bread got up and walked around to clear the drowsiness from her head. She peeked out the door, into the night. The soft light from the little fire outside flickered on the faces of Black Fox and Fighting Bear. Both were awake. That made her feel better. She came back to the hearth and sprinkled more tobacco. The spark appeared above the middle of the ashes. She peered up through the smoke hole and began to wonder what form this particular night-goer had taken. If it could fly over the house, it would not likely be a cougar. It might be an owl, or perhaps a little ball of purplish light. It could be a raven-mocker. Chestnut Bread shuddered at the thought. She began to wish she had someone to keep her company. It was not so reassuring anymore to know that Fighting Bear was outside guarding. With night-goers something could always go wrong. She wished Fighting Bear would come sit inside. What if a night-goer got in somehow while he was still out by the fire? What good would he be then?

Her ashes had grown cold, and she scraped them back into the fire and spread out some new ones. Easy Dancer had begun to snore lightly. Redbird turned in her sleep. Black Fox had been right when he said it was more frightening to watch alone. She sprinkled tobacco over the ashes. Two sparks. Another night-goer had come. Both were behind the house, probably hiding in the trees. She wondered if they were working separately of if they were conferring together, plotting a way to get in. Could there be others on the way? Maybe Redbird was getting so weak that night-goers from all over were sniffing her out. Maybe the house would soon be surrounded by hordes of the horrible creatures, and maybe one among them would be powerful enough to get in.

Outside a dog suddenly began to bark. Her heart went cold with fear. She took another pinch of tobacco and sprinkled it over the ashes. Three! One behind the house, one where the dog was barking, one over the house! Her hand trembled as she added more sourwood to the fire. Fighting Bear should come in! What if he waited until the last moment and then his bad leg kept him from making it in time? She sprinkled more tobacco over the ashes. Now there were *four*! Fighting Bear had to come in! He had to! She jumped up and ran to the door. "Fighting Bear!" she called.

In the firelight Fighting Bear slowly lifted his head and looked at her. Then, just as slowly, he raised his hand and pointed to the east. She looked and saw the dawn—the brightening of the darkness above the horizon. Her eyes closed in a sigh of relief.

"What is it, Little Daughter?" asked Easy Dancer from her bed.

Chestnut Bread turned back into the house. "It's all right," she said. "There were night-goers gathering, but they're too late. The dawn has come."

"Try the tobacco, Little Daughter."

Chestnut Bread drew out some hot ashes and sprinkled tobacco over them. There was no spark. None at all. "They've gone home," she said.

"That's good," said Easy Dancer. "The night is over." But it was still dark, and she was still weary. She settled back down and was soon sleeping again.

As Chestnut Bread sat down again, her thoughts turned to Soaring Hawk. Had he been able to overcome Scratcher during this long, lonely night? In her mind's eye she could see it happen that way. She could see Redbird waking up in the morning light, talking, smiling, maybe sitting up, and it would be plain to see that she was getting well at last. What relief they would all feel! What joy! They would begin to laugh again. They would all go down to the river and give thanks. It could happen that way. She knew it. How many times had she hoped very much for something and had her hopes come true? She knew the feeling. She could feel it now.

But just as many times, it had been fears that had come true instead of hopes. Suddenly she could imagine finding Redbird worse than ever when daylight came. She could feel the helplessness and despair that comes when hope has slipped away. The memories of death came flooding back to her. She managed to shake away all of them but one—the one she needed the most to forget. It was the memory of little Cornflower lying sweetly in her bed, crying now and then as she passed through her last day on this side of the Darkening Land. Chestnut Bread searched about in her heart for comfort, but at this moment there was none to be found.

Ten

High in the forest in their camp beside the mountain river, Soaring Hawk and Owl waited for yet another day to pass. The conjuring of the second night had also failed. Now it was apparent that it was going to take a third or even a fourth night to beat Scratcher. They sat listlessly by the river, away from the lean-to, for the fire in there could not be allowed to die and it was uncomfortable to be near it in the steamy heat of mid-day. Neither of them had said anything for a long time. Now Soaring Hawk broke the silence.

"Suppose someone had a dream about the Thunder Boys," he said. "What would you say it meant?"

"You haven't been dreaming, have you?"

"No! I mean, not lately. Not since we've been here. But the last time I dreamed, whenever it was—let's see . . . two nights of conjuring . . . the night before that—three nights ago. The last night I spent at home. I think I dreamed about them then."

Soaring Hawk was tired. After two nights without sleep he was beginning to have trouble coordinating his thoughts and his words. But he managed to sound coherent as he told Owl about his dream of the strange boys with snakes for necklaces, about how they had beckoned to him, trying to make him come close.

"It sounds to me like a warning of a false-likeness disease," said Owl.

"Yes, that's what I thought. I think that's what Fighting Bear would have said."

"You mean you didn't tell him about it?"

"There was so much happening the next day. I forgot it."

Owl rose from the rock on which he was sitting and went to the lean-to to light his pipe with a coal from the fire. As he came back he asked, "Have you decided what it means to you?"

"It's obvious, I think. When we thought Redbird was sick with fish spirits, it was really much more. It was a false-likeness. Scratcher sent it and made it look like fish spirits so that we would treat it the wrong way and let the thing get as far as it did before realizing what it was." Soaring Hawk paused. His face grew dark with hatred. "False-likeness disease," he said bitterly. "Such a vicious thing. I didn't know his heart was so black."

Owl puffed on his pipe and said nothing.

Soaring Hawk watched the smoke as it curled above Owl's head. For two nights he had failed in the conjuring. Half of his chances were used up. What could be wrong? Why couldn't he find the power? He kept asking himself that over and over. What could be wrong? Could it be Chestnut Bread? Had she deceived them? Could she be working against them? She could be taking reports to Scratcher—or even doing his work for him right there at Redbird's bedside. She could be. Why had he let her in? Why had he said she could stay? . . . Hateful, blackhearted snake! He hated her! He had to get her out of his house! He had to go home now and throw her out of his house!

He jumped to his feet, but even as he did his thoughts were dissolving again. New ones came marching in—tender thoughts of his lovely Chestnut Bread. How could he think such awful things about her? Hadn't she taken the rabbit he offered her? That was a brave thing for her to do right there in front of Scratcher after he had ordered her back into the yard. And hadn't she shown how strong-hearted and independent she was by telling him that story about one of her fathers? And what about the way she had hurried o kind and devoted. Her heart

t snow of winter. She was every-

had ever wanted in a woman, ev-

hoped for in a wife.

to tremble and he sat down again.

to do but keep his trust in her. He

ice on that first day when he asked

hat was true then was still true today.

was not his problem.

s it then? What could he do that would

ices when he worked against Scratcher

ar he had been outmatched. It was as

hat. Scratcher was more powerful than he

ld change it? What could he do that he

done?

as Owl put d___

up? It's hard   ipe and got up to

st not make it   e vigorously and

                                 ee how much of

ger. "A person   t Soaring Hawk

r cannot do," he   dchild. How do

s that all his life

y sister is dying.   He was tired,

and by a hateful   n anyone else

o nothing—*noth*-   being a medi-

much for her: I   dinary case,"

ghts without sleep   he could. "I

e of things; many   y sister back

o this much, then

anyway. So I think   s all about.

e me alone. I'll do   be as pre-

e is to it."   n. A good

wl, Soaring Hawk   sick per-

d up the mountain   above all

osed in around him   ed to re-

ence. He wished he   k on his

ken so harshly, for   a wave

ng mainly from his   st think

                                 away.

He was hungry all right—hung
there were hunger pains any
those after the second day. Bu
flashed through his head, and th
definitely appealing. He could hav
he had wanted to, just before sund
he could eat this evening and not
power. He wondered if Scratcher
tonight.

Suddenly Soaring Hawk came alive.
it! If Scratcher ate tonight and he did
would make a gain in power where Sc
none. Perhaps it would be enough to tip the

He turned to Owl. "I'll go out and try
thing for you to eat, but as for me, I
break the fast."

"Don't be foolish, Grandchild," O
sharply. "How do you expect to hol
enough to go without sleep. You mu
harder on yourself than it has to be."

Soaring Hawk felt a surge of an
should not tell another what he can o
said coldly, barely controlling feeling
he had learned to keep in check. "M
She is being driven to the Darkening
enemy, and I have been able to d
ing—to stop it. Well, I can do this
can endure for four days and four ni
or food—it is nothing in the measur
men have done more. If I cannot d
life for the Deer people is hopeless a
other people would do well to leav
what I have to do, and that is all the

Without even looking again at O
strode out of the camp and heade
along the river trail. The solitude cl
and he felt at once its soothing influ
had left sooner, before he had sp
he knew that his anger had spru

hunger and his lack of sleep. He would have to try harder from now on; he would have to keep in mind that he could no longer trust his emotions.

Soaring Hawk headed upstream toward no particular place, though he thought of the falls that lay far ahead. He had seen them once, long ago, with Fighting Bear. The three of them had made the trip together, he and Fighting Bear and Redbird. . . . Redbird. Suddenly Soaring Hawk was trembling with fear. Fear that Redbird would die. Fear that he could not save her. He fought against the terror and pushed it back. He had to keep from thinking of her. He would not give in to despair.

He forced himself to think only of where he was, here on the mountainside, alone with the water. As he walked along the river's edge, Long Man's song began to fill his heart, and for a while he felt soothed and comforted.

Then weariness began to take hold, and soon it was pulling at him, dragging at his feet, clouding his mind. Every large rock reached out for him and begged him to sit down and rest. But he knew to resist. He could not risk falling asleep even for a moment, for then he would lose his power and Scratcher would defeat him in an instant. And so he kept on walking, concentrating now not on the river but on simply staying awake. He tried shaking his head, rubbing water on his face, slapping his cheeks, pinching himself; he broke off a slender branch of a sapling, stripped off its leaves, and switched his legs as he walked along. It was a tortuous struggle, sheer agony not to be able to give in to a great desire to stop and close his eyes. If he could just rest his eyes. . . . But he knew that trick. If he closed his eyes, sleep would be there to slip in before he could wrench them open again. He thought of turning back to the camp, but there was nothing to do back there but sit around and wait for midnight. So he kept on walking, going higher up the mountainside, following the river trail.

Since the day before, strange things had been popping in and out of the edges of his field of vision. Tricks of sleepless eyes. He knew to expect them and they did not bother him—if anything, they entertained him. But now it was getting worse. Straight ahead he saw a little man stooped over tending a snare trap; but as he moved closer, the man became a bush, the snare a drooping branch. He shook his head and kept on walking.

After a time he saw a raccoon sitting in the path ahead not making the least attempt to flee at his approach. Yet when he drew near, it dissolved into a cold gray rock that did not look very much like a raccoon at all. It was at times like this that one could sometimes see Little People and Immortals and Thunder People and who knows what other elusive beings from the depths of the mountains and the shadows of the forest. They always knew when one's mind was confused, when eyes were untrustworthy, when alertness was lagging. If they felt playful they would show themselves just to fool a person and confuse him all the more.

But Soaring Hawk was sure he was not confused; he was in full control of his mind and could think his way through any problem put before him—in fact, if he were to put his mind to thinking all the way through some specific topic, it would be a good way to amuse himself and chase away the sleepiness. Now, what could he think about that was happy and entertaining? Well, the New Corn Festival, of course. What else at this time of year?

The festival. Soon, everyone would be giving up normal activities and working only on getting ready. The women would be busy cooking. And what good food! For the first feast they would use up the food left over from last year's harvest. It would be fixed so many different ways, each dish more delicious than the other. He always wondered why his mother waited for the festival to make that tired old food so exciting. But of course it was a lot of trouble, and she was so busy the rest of the year. If only there were other women in the lineage to share the work, as at Chestnut Bread's. Her homestead was always full of people. There were always one or two women with nothing else to do but cook. No wonder they ate so well.

Soaring Hawk walked along. After a while, he began to realize that his mind was wandering. How long ago had it left the festival? This was supposed to be a disciplined exercise in thinking and yet he had hardly gotten started before his mind took its own trail—the food trail. He struck his legs with the branch and decided to try again.

Festival. Think about the festival. Forget the food. That's the women's part, anyway. He would think about the danceground, where only the men could be. They were very strict about that during the festival. June Bug found it out the hard way. The guards dry-scratched him with blackberry briars for going inside the bounds of the danceground. He was not very old when it happened, so he could hardly be blamed for running in after his dog. Still, he was very brave to have done it—he knew he would be punished. The guards seemed to have thought it was brave, too, and that was probably why they didn't take the dog away from him and kill it. Of course, the dog never did know it had done anything wrong. It was only a puppy. Puppies don't know that only men are allowed inside the danceground during the festival.

Soaring Hawk wondered when they would say that *he* was a man. Some men never made it. They spent every festival of their lives beyond the danceground with the women and children. He could think of nothing worse. . . . Yes he could. Growing old without a lineage. Nothing could be worse than that.

Suddenly Soaring Hawk stopped in his tracks. Just ahead a bear cub was playing by the river. Another trick of his eyes? He looked away, then looked again. It was still there. He stared hard at it, and it did not

fade away. He squeezed his eyes shut and opened them
again. Nothing had changed.

Well, he decided, real or unreal, it would be fun to
watch a bear cub play. It would be something to
concentrate on, to hold his attention, and keep him
awake while he sat down to rest.

Soaring Hawk moved to a seat on a nearby rock and
settled down for the entertainment. At first the little
bear sported about on the bank, lunging this way and
that as it chased imaginary prey, but then, as if bored
with make-believe, it moved up to the water's edge to
try some fishing. Perching precariously on a rock, the
cub watched for a fish, made a quick swipe with its
paw, and came up with nothing. Looking for a better
position, it shifted around on the rock, teetering, but
not falling in. Soon it was watching the water closely,
waiting for another fish to come along, and when one
did it tried again and went tumbling into the water.
Soaring Hawk laughed to himself but the cub seemed
unconcerned and only started gallivanting about,
splashing and rolling around in the shallow current.

As Soaring Hawk watched, a strange feeling began
to come over him. It was as if he were somehow ceas-
ing to exist, as if all that was here was the cub and the
stream, the rocks and the trees and the moss, the birds
and the insects, and the sunlight shimmering through
the leaves as they rustled ever so slightly in the warm
breeze. The jaybirds were fussing to warn the smaller
animals of the cub's presence, not the cub of him because he was not there. He was watching from beyond
This World, perhaps from the Upper World above the
dome of the sky. He felt privileged to have this oppor-
tunity to view the forest in its true beauty, as it was
when there was no man there to disturb its tranquillity.

There was beauty in the cub as it splashed and
played in the cool, clear stream. There was beauty in
the jaybirds screaming in the trees and in the squirrel
scampering up a rough-barked tree trunk into a leafy
refuge. There was beauty in the mother bear coming

into the stream's clearing from the forest, rising now to sniff the air for danger to her cub, falling again to all fours and lumbering closer to the water. The cub gave a little squeal of delight to see its mother, and as if showing off in front of her, it threw itself into the water after a fish and surprisingly came up with it.

Soaring Hawk watched her as if he were not there. She raised up on hind legs again and sniffed the air and looked curiously in his direction. He wondered what had caught her eye. She could not be looking at him. He was the same as a rock or a bush or a tree: He was not there at all. She fell on all fours and started toward him, slowly, heavily. It did not occur to him to be afraid. Instead he was fascinated by her. He had never seen a live bear up so close—at least not one that he was not about to kill. He looked at her thin, scraggly coat. That was her summer coat, of course; in the winter it would be much thicker. She saw him looking at it and drew up on her hind legs so he could see it better. But now he was studying her face. It was the moisture that caught his eye. He had never before noticed all the moisture on a bear's face. Her small eyes glistened. Her nose looked cold and moist, like the underside of a half-buried stone that had just been turned up from the earth. Her saliva hung in silvery threads between her top and bottom teeth, and every now and then a drop spilled down on her chest, making little beads that glistened on her fur. In a moment she would be close enough for him to smell her breath. He had always heard that a bear's breath had a horrible, stifling smell.

The she-bear stopped for a moment, swaying on her hind legs, and then she gave a low, menacing growl. The sound of it struck Soaring Hawk's ears like a clap of thunder! The forest plunged into a dizzying spin and a dull roar filled his head as reality came rushing back and he stood frozen with terror. Then from the depths of his being came what was surely the loudest and most horrible yell he would ever in his whole life be capable of giving. The bear had never heard anything like it, and with a startled yelp she turned and fled. But Soaring Hawk did not see her go, for he too was running, plunging headlong down the river trail.

He ran when he knew he no longer had to run, but somehow he could not command his legs to stop. Finally, upon rounding a bend in the trail, he whizzed past Owl, who barely managed to jump out of his way. By the time he could bring himself to a halt, he was a good way down the trail, and Owl walked down to meet him.

"Going somewhere?" the old man called ahead.

Soaring Hawk leaned weakly against a tree, panting, and watched old Owl come toward him. What a story he had to tell! As he held his stomach and gasped for breath, a feeling of hilarity began to rise within him. It made his eyes water and he began to chuckle and then to laugh. He laughed and laughed until Owl was chuckling too. Finally Soaring Hawk managed to regain his composure.

"What's so funny?" asked Owl with a grin.

"Nothing," said Soaring Hawk, "except that I almost got killed by a bear. I've never been so scared in all my life. But when I get home and tell the story around the fire, I know what's going to happen. Everybody's going to laugh until they fall over. I think I would too if I heard it from somebody else."

"Tell it to me and see if I do," said Owl.

"I will tonight, Grandfather. After you've eaten we can sit at the fire and tell stories. It will help us stay awake."

"I'm not eating tonight," said Owl. "That's what I was coming to tell you."

Soaring Hawk looked away with embarrassed pleasure. It seemed that old Owl was going to stand beside him after all. Together they turned and headed down the river trail to their camp.

Eleven

Darkness had fallen and the mountain air was growing cool. Inside the lean-to, in a tiny circle of firelight, Soaring Hawk spoke softly as he related to Owl his encounter with the bears. If Owl had been home in the village when he heard it, he would have whooped with laughter in a way that would have hearkened back to his younger days. But in the lonely camp deep in the mountain forest, he just leaned back on one elbow and let his laughter roll out gently and quietly, the thousand wrinkles on his face crinkling up in old man's mirth. So soft was his laughter and so loud the rushing water of the river that Soaring Hawk could only *see* him laugh. He thought the old man looked beautiful there against the darkness with the firelight dancing on the white paint designs that covered his body.

At last Owl's merriment subsided enough for him to speak. "Now you have your own bear story," he said. "I'm glad it's funnier than the one your uncle tells."

"I am too," said Soaring Hawk. "For a moment I thought it was going to be more tragic. I was not even sure I'd be around to tell it. Did you hear me yell?"

"No. The river is so noisy; it blocks out a lot. And I was pretty far away."

"Well, that bear wasn't. She's probably still wondering what she ran into."

The two began chuckling again. Then they grew quiet, and for a time they listened to the night, to the songs of the frogs and the whippoorwills and to a screech owl that trilled softly in the distance. At last

Owl reached for a coal to light his pipe, and Soaring Hawk knew he was getting ready to tell a story of his own.

"This is not going to be about bears," said Owl, "but it's something I remembered when you told me your dream this morning. It's a story about a man who married Thunder's sister, and it was told to me by my grandmother, who said it was true. And here is what she told me:

"Once there was a dance in Mulberry Town, which as you know is not far from here on one of the head-streams of our river. After this dance had started, two young women with long, beautiful hair came in, but no one knew who they were or where they had come from. They danced with one partner after another, and in the early morning they slipped away before anyone knew that they were gone. But a young man from the town had fallen in love with one of the sisters, on account of her beautiful hair, and in the manner of our people he had already asked her through an old man if she would marry him and let him live with her. To this the young woman had replied that her brother at home must first be consulted, and they promised to return for the next dance seven days later with an answer; but in the meantime, she had said, if he really loved her, he must prove his constancy by a rigid fast until then. The eager lover readily agreed and impatiently he counted the days.

"In seven nights there was another dance. The young man was on hand early, and later in the evening the two sisters appeared as suddenly as before. They told him their brother had consented to the marriage and that after the dance they would conduct him to their home, but they warned him that if he told anyone where he went or what he saw, he would surely die.

"He danced with them again and about daylight the three left the town just before the dance closed, so as to avoid being followed, and started off together. The women led the way through the woods along a trail the young man had never noticed before. After a while they came to a small creek, and without hesitating, the two sisters stepped into the water. The young man paused in surprise on the bank and thought to himself, 'They are walking in the water; I don't want to do that.' The women knew his thoughts as if he had spoken and turned and said to him, 'This is not water; this is the road to our house.' He still hesitated, but they urged him on until he stepped into the water and found it was only soft grass that made a fine, even trail.

"They went on until the trail came to a large stream which he knew was Briar Town River. The women plunged boldly in, but again the young man hesitated on the bank, thinking to himself, 'That water is very deep and will drown me; I cannot go on.' They knew his thoughts and turned and said, 'This is not water, but the main trail that goes past our house. Our house is very close now.' He stepped in, and instead of water there was tall waving grass that closed above his head as he followed them.

"They went on only a short distance and came to a rock cave close under the high falls of the river. The women entered, while the young man stopped at the cave's mouth; but they said, 'This is our house; come in, our brother will soon be home; he is coming now.' They heard low thunder in the distance. The young man went inside, but remained close to the entrance. Then the women took off their long hair and hung it up on a rock, and both their heads were like pumpkins—as smooth as any pumpkin you have ever seen. 'It is not hair at all,' the man thought, and he was more frightened than ever.

"The younger woman, the one he was about to marry, then sat down and told him to take a seat beside her. He looked and saw that the seat was a turtle, which raised itself up and stretched out its claws as if angry at being disturbed. The young man said it was a turtle and refused to sit down, but the woman insisted that it was a seat. Then there was a louder roll of thunder, and the woman said, 'Now our brother is nearly home.' While they urged, and he still refused to come nearer or sit down, there suddenly came a great thunderclap from just behind him, and turning quickly he saw a man standing in the doorway of the cave.

" 'This is my brother,' said the woman, and the brother came in and sat down upon the turtle, which again rose up and stretched out its claws. But the young man still refused to come in. The brother suggested that the young man might like to see his finest hunting dog; he sent his sister to bring it in. She went out and soon came back leading a great uktena snake that curled and twisted along the whole length of the cave. 'Come play with it,' she said, but the young man was terribly frightened and answered, 'That's a snake; I can't play with that!' The others insisted that it was no snake, but their friendly hunting dog.

"The brother grew impatient with the young man and said to his sisters, 'Maybe he would be happy if you brought him some bracelets for his wrists and arms.' The women went out and came back with some armbands. But the bracelets were living slimy snakes, and the women were about to twist them around the young man's wrists.

"Now he was almost dead with fear. 'What kind of horrible place is this?' he said. 'I can never stay here and live with snakes and awful things.' The brother got very angry and called him a coward, and then it was as if lightning flashed from the brother's eyes and struck the young man, and a terrible crash of thunder stretched him senseless.

"When at last he came to himself again, he was standing with his feet in the water with both hands grasping a laurel bush that grew out from the bank, and there was no trace of the cave or the Thunder People, but he was alone in the forest. He made his way out and finally reached his own town, but found then that he had been gone so long that all the people had thought him dead, although to him it seemed to be only the day after the dance. His friends questioned him closely, and he forgot the sisters' warning and told the story. But in four days he died, for no one can come back from the Under World and tell it and live."

Owl fell silent, and for a long time Soaring Hawk sat lost in thought. He felt close to the young man in the story and so taken with his strange experience that he somehow could not let go of it. It was only when Owl moved to put another stick of wood on the fire that the real world came back to him. He noticed then that the moon had risen and that it was casting pale highlights on the river. It was as if Long Man himself had put on white paint.

"What if the young man had not told anyone?" he asked.

"I suppose he might have lived to be an old man," said Owl.

"Do you really think all of that happened to him? Do you think it was real or was it a vision?"

"Is a vision not real? Was the stream a trail, or was the trail a stream? How can you ever know what is real and what is not?"

"I saw things today that weren't real. I saw a raccoon that was not real—it was only a rock."

"Was it a vision then? A vision of a raccoon?"

"Hardly," grinned Soaring Hawk. "At least that's not what I thought a vision was supposed to be like."

"Have you never had a vision, then?"

"I don't think so."

"If you had one, you would know it. And the question of real or unreal would not even occur to you."

"I guess you've had a lot of experience with visions."

Owl did not reply at once. When at last he did speak, it was in a voice so hushed that Soaring Hawk could barely hear him. "Grandchild," he said, "I have seen the whole universe laid out before me. I have seen it all at once like a valley from a mountaintop." Owl's wrinkled eyelids slowly closed. "I have seen the four edges of This World and the waters beyond. I have seen the sky dome that covers it all like a bowl turned over a hearthstone to bake bread. I have seen the Upper World above the sky dome. It is a beautiful world—like this one, only much grander. When the sun sets in This World, it goes down beneath the edge of the sky dome and comes up on the other side. It is rising in the Upper World then. The animals are larger up there and have more power, and everything is in perfect order. But the Under World is not like that. I know, because I have seen it too. It is filled with dark pools and mountain caverns. Some caverns have meadows and towns, but others are black and cold with uktenas and monsters living inside. The seasons are backward down there. Our people have always suspected they were backward because all the rivers and streams flow from there and the waters are always cold in summer and warm in winter. I can tell you here tonight that our people are right about that—I have seen that it is so. But there are stranger things than that down there, stranger than our people could ever imagine. Nothing down there is like we know it here."

Owl fell silent and seemed lost in thought. Then he said, "I have seen all times at once, as if I were far above on a cloud looking down on everything. I have seen my own birth and also my death. I have seen my white bones stored away in their special place. I have seen my grandmother as a baby at her mother's breast. I have seen ancestors of mine who lived so long ago that we have forgotten their names, and I have seen my descendants who will live in days to come. I have seen our people coming long ago from the west to live here in these mountains, and I have seen strangers coming from the east to conquer us long after I am dead. Grandchild, I have seen so much that I could never find the words to tell it. This is the first time I have ever spoken of these things to anyone."

Soaring Hawk was stunned. It was the most marvelous vision he had heard of in his life. And to think that he was the first ever to be told anything about it. What could he say that would be even remotely appropriate?

But old Owl did not seem to expect anything from him, and after a while the old man spoke again. "All I have wanted to do since then is think about the things I saw. At first I could find no peace at all. My nieces bothered me. They asked too many questions. It seemed that everyone wanted me to be like I was before—but how could I? I had seen too much to ever be the same. Finally I just moved out, cut myself off. It was the right thing to do. I needed those long years alone. But now I think it is time to pass what I have learned to someone else. It will take a long time. There is so much to tell. . . . It is not knowledge for everyone to have. It is powerful and I'm still not sure how it is meant to be used. But this much I am sure of: This great knowledge was intended for the benefit of our people, and that is why it was given to me."

Owl fell silent and said nothing more.

"There is no ulunsuti crystal then," Soaring Hawk heard himself say. He was at once embarrassed that his first response should be so trifling.

"I'm sure there is somewhere," replied Owl seemingly unoffended, "but not in my possession. My mother knew a man who had one, but I don't know what became of it."

Soaring Hawk thought it best not to try to say anything more. He stretched out on his back and gazed up at the drying boughs that covered the roof frame of the lean-to. The implications of what he had just heard were racing through his mind. Was *he* the one Owl was going to give his knowledge to? Owl said he saw everything. Had he seen what was going to happen to Redbird? Had he seen the man Chestnut Bread would marry? Could he ask him things like that?

"You haven't gone to sleep, have you?" said Owl.

"No, Grandfather."

"Do you think it's time to start the curing?"

"Yes, it is time. . . . I feel different, Grandfather. I feel that something has changed. Perhaps Scratcher will get a surprise tonight." He brushed himself off as he got to his feet. "Have you noticed Long Man?" he asked, nodding toward the river. "He is wearing white paint tonight."

Twelve

Soaring Hawk sat slumped against a tree watching through tired eyes as the gray light of dawn filled the mountain forest. Fog hung so heavily in the trees that the forest seemed cast adrift, a floating world filled with the songs of birds rejoicing at another day. But to Soaring Hawk it was not just another day. It was the last day of hope. He had just failed against Scratcher for the third night, and if nothing changed before the fourth night came, the sun would never rise again on a white and happy world. His beloved sister would die, and his life would be black and sorrowful, filled with loneliness, empty of purpose.

It did not seem possible that three of his four chances were gone. Yesterday at this time two nights had been used up, but two had remained, and success had seemed to him just a matter of time. Now suddenly time had turned from friend to enemy, and he had only one night left. In the gray morning light Soaring Hawk felt frightened and powerless. His world was coming down around him and it seemed now that there was nothing he could do.

Last night he had been so sure that something had changed, that at last his power would prevail over Scratcher's. But when he began to conjure, he saw that if there had been any change at all, it was to Scratcher's advantage. The bead that was Redbird had done no more than tremble in Owl's fingers while the black one danced triumphantly in the other hand.

Tonight perhaps the red bead would not even tremble. Soaring Hawk nearly wept at the thought.

He looked over at Owl sitting calmly in the lean-to, puffing endlessly on that pipe of his. What good is he, Soaring Hawk wondered angrily. He is supposed to be so powerful, his knowledge so valuable, but what good has he done me? How do I even know he is holding the beads right? Maybe he's too old to do it anymore.

Soaring Hawk heaved a deep sigh. I should have come alone, he thought wearily. I should be here by myself, all alone with only the birds. Just the birds and the river and the fog. . . .

Soaring Hawk felt himself nod, the morning fading out and then in again. He started. Had he gone to sleep? It was hard to know, but he did not think he had. He had come close, though—close enough to make it clear that he could not remain in camp and hope to stay awake. He would have to get up and walk—walk without stopping. That would be the only way to make it through the day without sleeping. He felt himself nod again. He shook his head sharply. He had to get moving now, before it was too late. As he rose to his feet, his legs wobbled and almost gave way. The world swayed for a moment, and he reached for the tree to steady himself.

"I think someone needs to take along a walking stick," Owl said from the lean-to.

"Yes . . . a walking stick," murmured Soaring Hawk, wondering how the old man knew he was about to leave. He would have said more, like where he was going or how long he would be gone, but his tongue felt thick and slow. Or was it his mind that was now so sluggish? Whatever it was, it felt better not to talk. After cutting a good, sturdy stick, he waved with it to Owl and started on his way.

He headed upstream along the same trail he had taken the day before. As the sun rose higher, the fog began to lift, and the beauty of the morning crept into his heart and made it ache.

Before long the fog had lifted altogether, and the sunshine poured down into the narrow hollow that cradled the fast-moving river. Soaring Hawk looked up at the wooded mountains that rose above him on either side, and he began to feel that he was in a separate world, a world so small that it was bounded by the limits of his vision—a separate world in which he was the only inhabitant. He felt like Lucky Hunter, the First Man, and he wondered where Corn, the First Woman, might be. Maybe she was waiting for him up ahead.

He walked along the trail until he came by a place in the river where the water had cut out a little pool as it rushed around a boulder in its path. The pool was not so very deep but it was enough for him to get wet all over, and that would help him stay awake. Dropping his walking stick on the bank, he slipped into the water. It was so cold, it took his breath away. He didn't linger, for he only meant to get wet, and soon, walking stick in hand and water dripping from his body, he was on his way up the mountain again.

He soon passed the place where the day before he had met the bears, but he pushed on, following the stream, climbing higher and higher up the trail. His mind wandered aimlessly. For a while he thought only about his legs pushing him up the mountain, and then he had no thoughts at all. He lost track of time. After a while the river's song began weaving its way through his heart, faintly at first, but growing louder and more persistent. Now and then he heard in it something he thought he recognized, something that sounded familiar. Could it be his name? Yes, his name. Long Man was talking to him. He could hear his name. But what else? Something was being said that he should hear. Why couldn't he understand?

The day wore on and the trail grew steeper until at last he was not far from the falls. The falls—had he known all along he would go that far? Was that perhaps his destination when he started out? It was a long walk for someone in his condition. He had probably been foolish to come. What if he became too exhausted to get back to camp again? What would happen to Redbird then? But the river's song kept washing over him, carrying away his doubts, and though extremely weary, he continued on, leaning heavily on his stick. Before long he heard a low rumbling like thunder up ahead. The farther he went, the louder and more compelling the thundering song grew, until finally, over a rise, he saw the falls. The sight stopped him in his tracks, his mouth open, his heart pounding: Never before had they seemed so splendid, so magnificent, so awesome. The sight overwhelmed him and seemed to drain away what little energy he had left. As he walked the last short stretch of his journey, his head was swimming and his feet felt as heavy as the great black logs that lay scattered among the rocks and debris at the foot of the falls.

With tortuous effort he climbed toward the cascading water until at last he felt a cool mist blow over his body. He stopped and looked up and felt his strength return as if some medicine man had sprayed him with a healing potion. In the falls he could see Long Man towering over him clothed from head to foot in a shimmering robe of white. As he stood marveling, he noticed the great rock wall behind the water, and in the wall he saw a deep crevice that ran back into the mountain—not to darkness but to soft light, as if somewhere inside a fire were burning. With his new strength he moved quickly forward, scrambling over rocks and logs until he reached a low rock ledge just above the water's surface. The ledge ran back behind the falls, and Soaring Hawk followed it until he reached the crevice. Without a moment's hesitation, he slipped inside.

In the next instant he found himself in a vast meadow, and he was cold. Snow was falling softly and it covered the ground, though not deeply. He shivered. Far in the distance he saw a solitary homestead with smoke wafting gently from a warm winter house. As he moved toward it, the distance seemed to fall away, and he reached the homestead almost at once. A woman came out from the winter house, a beautiful young woman with soft, golden skin. She beckoned him to come in and she stepped aside so he could enter. She followed him inside, but when he looked at her in the firelight, he was startled to behold an old woman, bent and wrinkled.

He saw then that he was standing in the center of a great townhouse, larger than any he had ever seen. The seats all around were filled with people, and the rumble of their voices as they talked among themselves was like low thunder, like the sound of a waterfall. He was still cold and shivering, and he moved closer to the fire, but instead of warmth the fire gave off a cold draft that chilled him even more. Then a child came forward offering a wet blanket. Soaring Hawk understood, and taking it, he wrapped it around himself and found it as warm as a bear skin with the fur side turned in.

A townhouse attendant passed him a bowl of black tea that looked and smelled like the tea the men back home drank before convening council, but Soaring Hawk politely refused it, feeling thankful that he had enough of his wits about him to remember that if he ate or drank in the Under World, he could never go home and expect to remain alive. With a knowing smile the attendant removed the cup.

Now a great silence fell over the room. The head medicine man rose and opened the council with a long song. Soaring Hawk could not understand the words, but the music was beautiful, like rain falling through the leafy boughs of a summer forest. When the medicine man finished, the chief's speaker stood up and introduced the chief, who rose from his seat with great dignity. He turned at once to Soaring Hawk, who was still standing alone before them all in the center of the great hall.

"Why have you come?" the chief asked in a voice as

light as a tiny stream, not at all like the booming thunder Soaring Hawk had expected.

"Redbird, my sister, is sick and I am trying to cure her," he said.

"Who is afflicting her?" the chief asked.

"Scratcher of the Wolf clan."

The chief returned to his seat, which Soaring Hawk now noticed to be a great turtle. "You must be very tired after all your fruitless labors," said the chief. "Won't you stay the night? Tomorrow we can discuss this matter further."

Soaring Hawk was suddenly overcome with great weariness, and the urge to sleep through the night was becoming irresistible. He allowed the old woman to lead him out of the townhouse into the snowy night. He looked back and the townhouse appeared again to be only a small, family winter house, and when he looked now at the woman, she was once again young and beautiful. Then he saw that she was taking him to a crude lean-to, cold and drafty with no fire in it. He balked. He would freeze to death in such a place. The woman seemed to read his thoughts. "It is our winter house," she said. "You will find it very warm." When he entered, he did indeed find himself in a winter house, and where the hearth should have been there was a small pool of water that gave off such warmth that he would have no need for even a blanket. He turned to thank the young woman, but she was gone. He went to the door and looked out and saw a bent old woman tottering back to the townhouse. He stepped back inside, and lying down on a bunk against the wall, he fell immediately into a deep and dreamless sleep.

When he awoke and looked outside, he was still in the same place, but the morning and most of the afternoon had already passed. The snow was still falling, but on the ground it seemed no deeper. The woman was young again as she came across the yard to lead him back to the townhouse. He went willingly and found himself standing again in the center of the great meeting house of the Thunder People. This time the attendant offered both food and drink, but even though Soaring Hawk was experiencing great hunger, he refused again as politely as he knew how. As the food was carried away, his hunger somehow went with it, and he felt as satisfied as if he had eaten.

After what seemed a longer delay than the evening before, the head medicine man sang the opening song and the speaker again introduced the chief. As the chief rose to his feet, the great turtle on which he had been seated began to move, as if to leave. A light touch from the chief's speaker made it still again, though its neck remained stretched out and its eyes seemed to glare. Distracted by the turtle, Soaring Hawk was a little startled to find the chief addressing him.

"We are all amazed," the chief was saying, "that one so young has come into the mountains all alone to work such an important cure."

"Actually, I'm not alone," said Soaring Hawk. "Owl of the Paint clan is with me."

A low murmur spread through the townhouse.

"We all know of Owl," said the chief. "He is a very powerful man."

"That is true. But he is only serving as my assistant."

Now there was laughter from the crowd.

"It does not matter what you call him," the chief said. "His power always comes with him. If he works for you, his power does too. Now, who is it you said is strong enough to stand against Owl?"

"Scratcher of the Wolf clan."

The chief took his seat. "You have labored hard to overcome Scratcher," he said. "You must still be very weary from your futile efforts. Won't you stay the night? We can discuss this matter further tomorrow."

Soaring Hawk *was* tired, even though he had already slept so long. The invitation was too tantalizing to refuse, and once again he was taken to the lean-to, where he slept warmly through the night and through most of the following day.

When he was returned to the townhouse, he again refused food and drink and waited patiently for the chief to reconvene the council. Finally the head medicine man sang the song, the speaker introduced the chief, and the chief once again rose to his feet.

"We have all been wondering," he said, "what you have done to get such an enemy as Scratcher."

"He called my uncle a weak man," said Soaring Hawk. "He said that my uncle brought too much rain for the young plants and that the crops would be lost. He stirred up the people with his talk, but then my uncle performed a very difficult ceremony and stopped the rain while still leaving enough to avoid a drought. Scratcher was wrong in his accusations and everyone laughed at him."

"And is it for this little thing that he undertakes to destroy your whole lineage?"

"Yes," said Soaring Hawk. "Before this we had not believed that his heart was black, but now it seems that it is."

"You still look very tired from your fruitless efforts," said the chief, taking his seat again. "Why don't you stay another night? We will discuss this further tomorrow."

Soaring Hawk could not understand why he should still be so exhausted, but there was no doubt that he was, and once again he gratefully accepted the chief's invitation. The woman that led him back to his sleeping quarters was still changing from young to old, but he no longer paid any attention. He stumbled inside to his bunk and collapsed upon it.

For the third time he slept through all of the night and most of the following day. The snow was still falling and still getting no deeper on the ground. The Thunder woman came and led him back to the townhouse, where he once again refused the food and drink that was offered to him. When the council was under way, the chief rose to speak.

"This man Scratcher seems to be a very powerful man," he said. "We have all been wondering if he is the head medicine man for your town."

"No, my uncle is."

"Your uncle must be weak for Scratcher to destroy him so easily. Perhaps Scratcher should be head medicine man."

"He would like to be."

"But isn't Scratcher a foolish man to think he could achieve such a position after showing such a black and evil heart?"

"I suppose so," said Soaring Hawk.

"A person who knows so much and can use his knowledge to change things should always think everything through very carefully," said the chief.

"What you say is true," said Soaring Hawk, "and Scratcher will surely learn this lesson, but I am afraid it will be too late for the Deer people."

"Yes, it is too late," said the chief, taking his seat again. "It is too late to continue this discussion. Why don't you stay another night and we will finish it tomorrow."

"Stay another night?" said Soaring Hawk. He was still very tired and looked around for the woman who always came to lead him to his bed. At first he did not see her, but when she moved toward him from the crowd, he gasped. It was Redbird! His heart pounded in his ears, and the room tipped and began to spin. Redbird reached out to steady him, but the hand that he grasped was the bony hand of the wrinkled old woman. She was not Redbird at all; she had only seemed to be. Yet it was enough to remind him that while he was sleeping through the peaceful nights in Thunder's winter house, his own beloved sister lay dying, or maybe she was dead already.

"No, thank you," he said to the chief. "I have stayed three nights already, and now I really must be going."

"Don't leave us," said the chief. "Stay longer."

"No, I can't. Thank you for your great kindness, but I must leave now."

"What is your hurry? There is no reason to go. Stay with us another night."

"There *is* a reason—by sister is dying!"

"You can do nothing against Scratcher. Stay with us. Attendant! Bring him some food!"

"No!" said Soaring Hawk. "I cannot give up now. I'm leaving!"

With that, he spun around and ran out of the building. He heard the Thunder People coming after him, but he did not look back. He ran as fast as he could across the vast expanse of meadow, but though his legs pushed hard, it seemed he was getting nowhere. Then suddenly a great rock wall loomed before him. He ran to it but nowhere in it could he see the crack through which he had entered. He stopped, his heart pounding. Behind him he heard the rumble of the Thunder People. But then he heard something else. Water! The sound of a waterfall! He ran along the wall toward the sound and came at last to the crevice. It was smaller now, just large enough for him to squeeze through.

As he started through it, someone spoke close beside him: "Soaring Hawk!" The voice was beautiful, like the river's song. He turned to look. There stood the woman—young and old, old and young. She seemed both ways at once, and both young and old seemed very beautiful. "We wish you well," she said. "Long Man speaks for us. We hope you will always hear him now. Do not tell of your visit here."

There was a bright flash of lightning and a crashing of thunder, and Soaring Hawk found himself standing dazed on the rock ledge behind the falls. As the mist from the falls fell on his face and revived him, a new feeling of panic arose within him. All around was darkness—it was night and there was no moon to light the path. How long had he spent in the Under World? He groaned aloud. Three nights and most of a fourth had passed since he had gone there. It was all too late. Scratcher had won his final victory, and Soaring Hawk had not even been there to give a fight. If Redbird was not yet dead, she would be by the time he got home. In grief and despair he slumped down onto the cold, wet rock.

But wait! What was time in the Under World? Things down there are never what they seem. What if in This World no more time had passed than what it took for the sun to go down? How could he know? He had to get back to camp! Maybe Owl would still be there! Maybe it was good that there was no moon, for that meant that the night was still young! Maybe there was still time after all!

In an instant he was up and on his way, slipping and stumbling in the darkness as he scrambled toward the path over the tumbled rocks and debris beneath the falls. The stars gave enough light to make a slight glimmer on the river, and he could hear the water as it rushed along its path. Guided only by these things, Soaring Hawk ran headlong down the river trail, stumbling and falling, scraping and cutting his knees and hands. Yet he never slowed his pace, for in his pounding heart a new strength had taken hold. It seemed to be coming to him from the Thunder woman, the woman who was young and old, whose voice was like the river's song.

Thirteen

The night could not have been old when Soaring Hawk left the falls, for by the time he stumbled into camp the moon had still not risen in the east. Owl was gone, but to Soaring Hawk's great relief the fire was still alive. It was still the night of the day he had left the camp, for if it were not, the fire would be dead. Owl would have either gone to look for him or else gone home for help; he would not have stayed in the camp nursing what would have been by then a useless fire.

Soaring Hawk added more wood and fanned up the flames, and then he went over to the stream's edge and sat on a rock with his feet in the water. He leaned down and let the cool water flow over the scraped and burning flesh of his hands, and he splashed his legs, washing away the blood and dirt and soothing the pain. He tried to gather his thoughts, to forget himself and his cuts and bruises. He pushed aside thoughts of his vision and what it meant to have visited the Under World. These thoughts could come another day. At this moment all his thinking had to be about Redbird.

He listened to the river, and at once it was talking to him, its song clearer now than it had ever been before. *Listen to your heart,* it sang. *Open your eyes and listen to your heart.*

Through the trees he could see the light of the rising moon. It was nearly time to conjure. Where was Owl? He needed the old man, he supposed. At least the Thunders seemed to think that Owl's power was working for him. But Soaring Hawk didn't really see how that could be. Fighting Bear's dream had clearly meant that *he,* Soaring Hawk, was the one to save Redbird. There had been nothing in it about Owl.

He stared into the water, watching it flow past him down the mountainside. *Think clearly,* it was saying. *Open your eyes. Listen to your heart.*

Soaring Hawk understood and began to ponder Fighting Bear's dream. *He,* Soaring Hawk, was outside the burning house. *He* was the only one in a position to do anything to save the ones inside. But Fighting Bear did not actually see him put out the fire. What if he had run to get someone to help him put it out? If he had, it would still be because of him that the family was saved.

You are waking up, Long Man sang. *Rub the sleep from your eyes.*

Then Owl's power *was* useful to him. But how could Scratcher stand against it? That had to be the next question. Had not the Thunders tried to point that out? "Who is strong enough to stand against Owl?" the chief had asked. And Soaring Hawk had answered that Scratcher was. But who was Scratcher, after all? He was a medicine man, true enough, and a good curer of arthritis. He was ambitious—too ambitious—and he was competing with Fighting Bear for power, and in that respect his heart might be red instead of white; but even so, red is noble. Red is not black, and no one had ever before seen a truly evil heart in Scratcher. Suppose, though, that Scratcher's heart *was* black. Could he stand even for a moment against Owl? Where in Scratcher could that kind of power be found? He did not have it.

As Soaring Hawk sat beside the river, all alone and shrouded in the darkness of the summer night, he suddenly saw very clearly what the Thunders were trying to tell him: *Scratcher was not the one.* He had wasted three nights working against the *wrong* man. The thought of it made him sick inside.

Who could be doing this? Who was powerful

enough? Who could strike down Fighting Bear with a single swift blow, muddle Soaring Hawk's mind so he could not see the truth, and stand unshaken against Owl's tremendous power? There was no one. It was impossible. Fighting Bear was the head medicine man in the town. No one was more powerful. No one, of course, except . . .

The idea, when it came, was an icy knife in his very soul. He sat shaken, his mouth open, his eyes fixed in an empty stare while all the pieces tumbled into place in his mind. It was Owl who had laughed at him when he failed in the cure the first night. Owl was the one who tried to make him eat and lose power. It was Owl who could so easily read his mind and keep him confused on the wrong trail. It was Owl who everyone said was a night-goer. Why had he ever tried to believe anything else?

Owl had tricked him from the start. The old man was too powerful. Soaring Hawk had never stood a chance against him—Redbird was doomed from the beginning. And where was Owl now? Probably gone back to the town, back to the Deer homestead, back to Redbird's bed, back to cut out her heart, eat her liver, suck away her breath and her soul. It was too late to stop him.

Soaring Hawk drooped with exhaustion. He should have felt agony, despair—but he felt nothing. There was only a terrible emptiness and an overwhelming desire to disappear from the face of the earth. The river rushed and sang, but he was listening no longer. His eyes fell shut and the night sounds swelled and roared in his ears, a mad jumble of wind in the treetops and water on the rocks, frogs and crickets and lonely whippoorwills. His body swayed and tipped; he did not try to control it; he felt he might be dying and he did not want to interfere.

Then came the hoot of an owl, soft and eerie, floating above the jumbled dissonance of the other night sounds. Soaring Hawk jumped to his feet in terror. For a moment the world seemed just as he had left it: cool night air, black forest silhouetted against a starry sky, mountain stream glimmering in the soft light of a newly risen moon. But then it came again. The cry of a night-goer owl, floating up along the river trail. Owl was coming back!

Soaring Hawk struggled to gather his wits. He had not expected the old man to return. What could he do to protect himself? There was not much time. Tobacco! Tobacco and hot ashes. Maybe that would help. He fumbled for the pouch on his belt. Gone! Where was it? For a moment his mind refused to think, as in dreams when his legs wouldn't run. But then he remembered. He had not taken his pouch with him that morning. He had left it by the fire. He ran to the lean-to. The otter pouch was gone! Where could it be? Had Owl taken it? What now? He was defenseless. What would happen when Owl got back and found him? Owl would be able to read his mind. He would know that Soaring Hawk knew everything. What would happen then? What would Owl do to him?

The owl—closer—hooted again. Seized with panic, Soaring Hawk turned to run. Then he saw the otter hanging in plain view on one of the poles that support-ed the roof of the lean-to—hanging where Owl had thoughtfully put it, up off the floor and out of the way. Soaring Hawk looked at the otter's eyes, and in the flickering firelight they were more hauntingly alive than ever. For a long moment he stood gazing into them. Then he reached for the pouch, and as he did, his fear slipped away and a great sadness washed over him. Clutching the otter to his heart, he fell to his knees and wept. He remembered the joy and hope he had felt on the day he made the pouch. It had seemed then that his life was a white trail stretching out before him—a river trail of knowledge and power and good things for his lineage. But now it had all turned black, and he was so powerless he could not even so much as name his enemy. His enemy was not Owl—beloved Owl. The

otter knew that, and in his heart Soaring Hawk did too.
Owl had not gone to steal Redbird's soul. He had gone
to look for him, for Soaring Hawk. The old man had
such a white and beloved heart that he even started out
without the moon to light the trails. The cry of the
owl came again, but Soaring Hawk paid it no mind. It
was only a bird. No night-goers were in these mountains tonight.

Before long the tears stopped, and Soaring Hawk sat
quietly by the fire, gathering himself together again.
Time was not going to stand still—he had to try the
beads again. But Owl was not there to help him, and
even if he were, whom would they try the beads
against? It would have to be someone powerful enough
to strike down Fighting Bear, and it would have to be
someone who knew enough to confuse a diagnosis. He
thought of the other medicine men and women in the
town, but none of them were as strong as Scratcher,
and all had better hearts.

It was while Soaring Hawk was pondering these
things and getting nowhere that Owl came back.

"Scratcher is not the one," said Soaring Hawk.

"I was hoping you would come to see that," said
Owl. "Who is it?"

"I don't know. Do you?"

"No," said Owl. "Where did you go today? I was
afraid you had walked too far and couldn't get back."

"I climbed to the falls," said Soaring Hawk. "I'm
sorry I caused you trouble."

Owl sat down with a weary sigh.

Soaring Hawk hesitated and then he spoke again.
"Grandfather, I've been wondering today about something you told me last night. You said you have been
to the Under World, and you described the things you
saw there. How could you tell me about it? Why won't
you die now in four days?"

"Don't worry, Grandchild. I am old, but I am not
ready to die. You see, I did not actually *go* to the Under World. I saw it from the high place where I was

standing. I saw everything from that one place. That is why I could tell about it. If I had gone to the Under World and been a guest there, then it would have been a different matter. Does that make sense to you?"

Soaring Hawk was silent for a moment. He knew now that he could never mention his vision to anyone, not even to Owl, for if he did so, he would die.

"I understand," he said. "I only wish it were so easy to understand who is attacking my lineage."

In the crowded summer house at the Deer homestead, in the dark corner that she had taken for her own, Chestnut Bread sat quietly alone. After the second night, when things had started to look bad, the friends of the Deer people began to arrive. They brought food, they cooked and cleaned, they carried water from the river, and they stayed through the third night and now through the fourth to help the Deer people guard against night-goers. Chestnut Bread watched them through the smoky haze, and she listened to the conversations that drifted in bits and pieces to her corner. She heard some people by the door pleading with Fighting Bear to call in other medicine men.

"Time is running out," they were saying.

"Soaring Hawk can't do it."

"Let someone else try."

If Fighting Bear was answering them, Chestnut Bread could not hear. Others in the room were talking about Scratcher.

"He hasn't been back since it all started," someone was saying.

The people talking were polite enough not to stare unkindly at Chestnut Bread, but still she knew their thoughts. Even those who did not think she was Scratcher's accomplice felt nevertheless that she was showing great disrespect for her father by being in the Deer homestead. Either way she lost; the only way to win would be to leave and go home, and it was probably too late even for that.

"She's near the end," someone was saying. One person or another had been saying that about Redbird all night.

Chestnut Bread sat in the shadows and stared despondently at the people as they milled about in the firelight. It was doubtful that Redbird could last the night. Everyone was saying so. Only Easy Dancer refused to admit it. "My son will save her," she said again and again. But anyone who looked at Redbird could see that she was close to death. Her eyes had sunk to an unnatural depth, and they stared at nothing, saw nothing. Her face was ashen and drawn and held no sign of life. From last night to this she had spoken only once, and this to Chestnut Bread.

It was because she was the only one who could still reach Redbird that Chestnut Bread did not go home. That was part of it, at least. She was also unshakable in her belief that she was carrying a trust from Soaring Hawk that could not be betrayed. She was determined to stay until they forced her to leave. Some had already tried to have her ousted—she had heard them talking—but Easy Dancer would not allow it. As she sat in her dark corner beyond the light of the fire, Chestnut Bread wondered sadly if she could somehow take Redbird's place in Easy Dancer's heart.

It was at that moment that she first heard the raven-mocker, and the sound of it sent a shock of terror into her heart. When it sounded a second time, the others heard it too—the cry of a raven diving and turning in the air; the cry of the most hideous of nightgoers, the unmerciful stealer of the hearts and souls of dead and dying people.

"No!" screamed Easy Dancer at the sound of it, and she threw herself over her daughter's body. As Black Fox rushed to stand by them, there was absolute panic in the house.

"Fighting Bear! Fighting Bear!" people were yelling.

"Where is he?"

"Where did he go?"

The raven-mocker cried again, so close now that people began running from the house.

"Wait! Make way!" cried a woman's voice, barely audible above the confusion. It came from just outside the door. "Stay where you are! Get out of our way!"

A few heard it and stopped, and then others, and still others. For a moment they stood motionless. Then Black Fox yelled, "Someone help her!" and a man ran forward to help Chestnut Bread as she struggled into the room with Fighting Bear leaning heavily on her. Crippled and haggard though he was, exhausted from pain and anxiety and sleepless nights, Fighting Bear nonetheless held the power to see the true identity of raven-mockers, and his very presence in the room was all that was needed to keep them away.

With great relief the people moved back inside, and the chatter and milling about resumed. As Chestnut Bread left Fighting Bear with the others and pushed through the throng, people smiled and patted her shoulder, but she quickly withdrew into the shadows, and sitting alone, she heard once again the pieces of conversations that drifted into her corner.

"Where had he gone?"

"A call of nature, I suppose."

"The raven-mocker must have been close by."

". . . watching for a chance."

"As soon as he stepped out . . ."

"I've never seen him so lame."

". . . could never have gotten back in time without her help."

"How did she move so fast?"

". . . only the second one I've ever heard."

"They say when one comes near, all other night-goers fly away like a covey of quail."

"It's probably still out there."

"Redbird must be nearly dead."

"Thank goodness she's not in pain."

"I doubt she will see the morning."

Chestnut Bread tried to stop listening. She sat with her chin on her knees waiting for the thunderstorm that had been brewing in the night sky when she ran out to find Fighting Bear. Soon she saw through the smoke hole the first flashes of lightning, and she could hear rumbling in the distance. Then came the scattered heavy drops striking the thatched roof; then the deluge, the bright flashes, the crashing thunder, and the hiss of stray raindrops that found their way through the smoke hole down to the sourwood fire.

On a rock by the river Soaring Hawk sat deep in thought. The night was wearing on, and several times Owl had suggested that they had better go on and do *something*, but each time Soaring Hawk said no. What good were the beads if he could not name his enemy? He was making progress, though. He knew he was. He was thinking more clearly than ever before, making a trail toward the truth. But the trail kept coming up against a rock wall.

He knew the enemy was not Scratcher, and it was not Owl, but it had to be someone powerful. Someone powerful enough to strike easily and swiftly with a blow that could leave Fighting Bear crippled and helpless and Redbird near death. Now who could do that? Who else knew things? Of the other medicine men, only Tall Pine came close in power, and he was weaker even than Scratcher. Besides, his heart was white. No one doubted that. Tall Pine was a fine man, a good friend of the Deer people.

So there was no one to suspect, no one that they knew, no one with a motive. Maybe it was a night-goer. Night-goers need no motives—they are driven only by an insane need to devour hearts and livers to add lives to their own. But why would a night-goer cripple Fighting Bear so that he could not leave the homestead? Just by being there Fighting Bear could protect Redbird from any night-goer, even from a raven-mocker. It would not make sense for a night-goer to operate in such a self-defeating way.

No one had the right combination of motive, power, and blackness of heart. Vengeful animal spirits had been ruled out long ago, and Redbird had not spit in Ancient Fire, or urinated in the River, or done anything to anger the Sun, or the Moon, or the Thunders, or any other of the world's forces.

Here was the rock wall again: it had to be *one* of these things—it could not be nothing at all. Nothing happened without a cause.

Open your eyes, Long Man was singing. *Consider everything. Think in new directions. Do not let yourself be tricked.*

Soaring Hawk knew that he *was* being tricked, that he had been from the very beginning. Nothing in this whole affair was obvious; nothing was what it at first seemed to be. It was like his vision, and like the dream he had of the Thunder Boys, the dream that had warned him of a false-likeness disease. He knew now that his interpretation of that dream had been wrong. It was not that this terrible thing had been sent to Redbird disguised as something caused by fish spirits—the fish spirit disease had been just what it had seemed. But someone had taken advantage of Redbird's weakness from it to strike her with a new illness. *Here* was the false-likeness—the new illness was made to seem so much the work of Scratcher that Soaring Hawk had never even thought to question it. The very danger of a false-likeness disease was that nothing was what it seemed to be. The clues would always lead down the wrong path.

As Soaring Hawk followed his thoughts, the night wind was gathering strength and blowing clouds across the sky to block out the stars and moon. A storm was coming, but he was oblivious to it. His thoughts were coming together now and he thought he had seen the rock wall shift. He knew now that his only chance lay in finding a new trail in his reasoning. He had to explore new directions, consider everything that was possible, look beyond the appearance of things.

Scratcher was out, and nobody else had a motive. And no night-goer could hope to get by Fighting Bear without being recognized and destroyed, no matter what form it might take—owl, raven, ball of fire, or even the form of a trusted neighbor or friend. Unless . . . unless that *was* its true form. Unless the night-goer really *was* someone the Deer people trusted, someone who could come in the house without a disguise. Now *there* was a real possibility! Soaring Hawk jumped to his feet as the wind whipped around him, bringing with it the first heavy drops of rain.

"It's someone in the house!" he cried to Owl.

"I'll get the beads," Owl said, and he went to fetch the otter pouch.

"But who? I still don't know who! It's someone who would come to help! . . . Chestnut Bread?" He gasped at the thought. "Oh, no! Not her! Grandfather, could it be her?"

The rain stung as it whipped about in the wind. "I hope not," Owl said softly. "She's of my clan." The old man slowly removed the beads and medicine skins from the pouch, and squatting in the rain, he laid them out on the bank.

Soaring Hawk grabbed up the otter and held it before him, looking hard into his eyes. "Otter, *you* know," he pleaded. "You saw her that day when I brought you from the winter house. Could it be that she is a night-goer? Has she worked her way into my house to kill my sister? What do *you* say about it, Otter?" The rain was starting to pour. Thunder rumbled through the sky. "No," murmured Soaring Hawk, "it's not her. That is just another false trail. It shows itself too easily." Lightning lit the sky and thunder followed closely. Soaring Hawk pressed his hands against his head as he tried to think. Suddenly he called out: "Help me, Thunder! I see now what you were trying to tell me in your townhouse! I have come this far with it!

Now show me who is killing my sister! *Which of my friends is my enemy?*"

The rain was pouring from the blackness overhead. As it fell through the trees it made a sound like the singer in Thunder's townhouse. It was the song that opened Thunder's council. Soaring Hawk turned his face to the sky and forced open his eyes against the rain. He was thinking of all the people who might be in his mother's house right now. One was a night-goer, and Thunder, the chief of the Thunder People, would tell him who it was. Soaring Hawk began to tremble; his hands trembled, his arms, his body, then his legs— they shook so violently that they began to give way beneath him. But Owl was there to catch him, to hold him up as the lightning cracked down with a blinding flash and the thunder crashed around them so violently that the whole mountain seemed to burst asunder. And in the midst of it Soaring Hawk saw his enemy, and he let out a cry of despair. He wanted to crumple in Owl's arms and never rise again. But instead his body straightened with some hidden strength, and though his anguish was terrible, he knew he could do what had to be done. He moved toward the beads.

"Did you see him?" he asked Owl. "Did you see who it was?" His own voice sounded strange and hollow.

"No," Owl said, "but I am sure you did."

Soaring Hawk took two of the beads, a red one for his right hand and a black one for his left. Owl did not come forward to take them, and Soaring Hawk did not offer them. He waded into the river, and facing upstream he held forward his arms, and between each thumb and forefinger, he held a bead toward the sky. Owl picked up the gourd rattle and began to shake it, and in the driving rain, with the thunder and lightning all around, Soaring Hawk sang the song to the red bead.

In his fingers the beads were moving and the red bead was at last showing strength and vigor. The black bead, so sinister and so accustomed to power, leaped into action when the song began, but almost immediately its movement began to diminish, slowly and steadily.

Then Soaring Hawk sang the next song.

"Hey, Black Bead! Listen while I call you.
Now you are coming down to us, you who never
  fail in anything.
Like the black cloud that rolls in with
  a thunder-storm
Your power is covering him.
Now his power is falling away from him
And the things he remembers are no good to him.
His power has become nothing.

"Hey, Black Bead! Listen while I call you.
Now you are coming down to us, you who never
  fail in anything.
Like the darkness of a black moonless night
Your power is covering him.
Now his black heart is exposed for all to see.
Now his sister drives him from her house.
Now the chief and all the people revile him.
His power has become nothing.

"Hey, Black Bead! Listen while I call you.
Now you are coming down to us, you who never
  fail in anything.
Like the terrible black water at the depth of a great
  whirlpool
Your power is covering him.
Now his black heart is pierced by my red arrow.
Now he crawls from the town like a wounded
  animal to die.
His power has become nothing.

"Hey, Black Bead! Listen while I call you.
Now you are coming down to us, you who never
  fail in anything.

Like the horrible black breath of a great uktena
Your power is covering him.
Now his soul is slipping away from him.
Now it has been carried to the Darkening Land.
It has been buried in black mud and covered with
*   a black rock.*
Now his soul is lost in the Darkening Land
And it will never return.
His name is Fighting Bear of the Deer clan!
His power has become nothing."

The black bead faltered altogether and it became as still as death.

Fourteen

Soaring Hawk and Owl waited for the storm to pass, and then, picking their way through misty darkness, they started down the mountain toward home. Soon the earliest birds of the morning began to sing, and as the dense fog was gradually illuminated by the dawn, the two quickened their pace, going swiftly and silently through the swirling whiteness. Soaring Hawk's feelings were as changing as the forms in the shrouded landscape that loomed large at his approach and then disappeared again into the mist. At times he was filled with horror and disbelief that Fighting Bear could actually be a night-goer and that having been recognized as one he was going to die within four days as surely as the sun would keep on rising. He tried to deny the reality, somehow to change in his mind the brutal fact that to save his sister and his lineage he had killed his uncle. But as suddenly as these feelings came over him, they would be lost again in the confusion of his exhausted mind. Then he would begin to feel stoic and manful, accepting with a grim fatalism this tragic turn in his life: Fighting Bear would be gone from their world, all memory of him erased, and after a time of adjustment, life would return to normal and go on as before. But just when he felt so much in control, his stoicism would be swept away by crushing sorrow. Yet even the sorrow did not stay with him, giving way instead to a numbing emptiness and the almost overwhelming desire to lie down and sleep. At times he would try to think about what it would be like when he came at last to the homestead, what he would say and do, but finally he gave up on this altogether. He would just have to do whatever the situation called for; he had no energy left to make plans.

By the time they reached the valley, the sun had risen over the mountains and the fog had disappeared. It was here on the outskirts of Raventown that Owl at last broke the long silence of their journey.

"This is where our paths divide, Grandchild. My dog and my owl are probably wondering if I am ever coming back. You go on now and face your homecoming with courage."

"I wish you would come with me, Grandfather. My mother will be expecting you. She'll have hot food for us. Please come, Grandfather. I want you to. Perhaps you can help us understand things."

Owl looked for a long time at the path that led to his lonely homestead. At last he turned to Soaring Hawk with a smile. "It's the food that tempts me," he said, and the two started out again, together.

When Soaring Hawk caught the first glimpse of his homestead, he stopped in the path with a groan. "Look at all the people in the yard. I was hoping they would be gone by now."

"Look who's with them," said Owl. "It's Fighting Bear."

"Where! What's he doing there?"

"I don't know. He's there by the fire."

"So he is," Soaring Hawk said softly. "I thought he would have crawled off to die by now. 'Like a wounded animal,' I said in my song. Why are they letting him stay? Do you suppose they still don't know about him?"

"That's what it looks like to me."

Soaring Hawk felt sick inside as they walked on. He had not expected this. He had been through too much already. He did not want to be the one to bring the terrible news. He did not want to stand among them and speak the words that would fill the homestead and the town with shock and anger.

When they came to the yard, Owl hung back, leaving Soaring Hawk to go on alone. People were smiling and shouting greetings at him, treating him like a returning hero. He looked at the ground as he walked past them, wishing fervently that they would all go away. He dreaded the moment that was rushing toward him, the moment when he would first see Redbird or Easy Dancer or Black Fox, for they did not know what he knew, and when they did, their hearts were going to break. He feared that when he saw them in their joy, he would lose the shaky hold he had on himself. He was so tired, so exhausted—how would he be able to keep back the tears? Fighting Bear stepped toward him, but without looking up Soaring Hawk pushed past him and ducked in through the door of the summer house.

Then he saw Redbird. She was sitting up. She was smiling at him with clear, bright eyes. She looked a little thin from her ordeal, but the women were giving her food, and she would soon be herself again. Soaring Hawk's heart turned white with joy, and he could only smile back—at her and at his mother and father.

But his joy was short-lived. The light fell from the doorway, and he knew at once who it was. He felt a rush in his head as he spun around to face Fighting Bear. The time had come to make his accusation. But before his words could come unstruck, Fighting Bear himself began to speak in a voice loud and clear so that everyone could hear:

"No one must think my nephew acted badly when he did not speak to me just then. He had good reason to treat me so. It is time now for everyone to sit and listen to what I have to say. I have asked Big Turtle, our beloved chief, to be with us today. He knows that what I will be saying is the truth."

Soaring Hawk had not noticed Big Turtle, but now he looked and saw him standing just beyond the doorway. People sat down where they were, inside and outside, but Soaring Hawk stayed on his feet. He had no idea what Fighting Bear was up to, and he was watching for a trick.

"As you all know," said Fighting Bear, "it was seven days ago that Redbird first fell ill. At that time she was correctly diagnosed and treated for fish spirits by her brother Soaring Hawk. Her recovery was rapid and it was a true credit to his medical skill. Then on the night before the last day of the cure, Redbird was stricken again, but this time it was by a false-likeness disease sent to her by someone in this town."

Fighting Bear paused and looked around. "*I* am that someone," he said.

The crowd gasped. There was excited talking and scattered shouts and cries. Easy Dancer stared in horror at her brother, and Redbird began to weep.

"No, my beloved niece," Fighting Bear said softly, "you must hold your tears until you have heard it all." Soon everyone was quiet and listening again. Fighting Bear said, "It is true that my niece has suffered much at the hands of her uncle, but let me assure her and everyone else that it was not done in malice.

"I am sure that at least some of you know that false-likeness diseases are not *always* sent by enemies or by night-goers." A few old men nodded, including Owl, who was standing alone at the edge of the crowd.

"My lineage is a small one," Fighting Bear continued, "so small that every day it is threatened with extinction. Right now it is guarded by my power, but the world has not been standing still for me, and I am getting on in years. When a man is no longer young, he thinks more and more that he will someday join his mothers in the Darkening Land. Then he wonders about the lineage he will leave behind. Will it be strong enough to survive? Will these two children, Soaring Hawk and Redbird, be able to overcome the great trials that men and women must face in this world? Can he keep her alive while she increases the lineage with children and raises them to adulthood? Will she have the strength to fight beside him, to hang on to life when others would let it go to escape the pain and suffering?

"These things have lately been much in my mind, and after great deliberation it was my decision that it would be a wise thing to test and strengthen my niece and nephew with an ordeal that would be as difficult as any they might ever encounter. That is why I sent the disease. It was a very difficult thing to bring such suffering to my beloved niece, and because of it I suffered great torture in my heart as I sat here watching her these last four nights. But though it was painful and hard, it was not foolhardy: As the sender of the thing I could withdraw it at any time and therefore I controlled the ultimate outcome. If Soaring Hawk had failed last night, Redbird would have still recovered. But I am proud to say that my nephew did not fail. Last night I felt his power shake loose the hold I had on Redbird. She is getting well this morning not because I arranged it, but because Soaring Hawk's knowledge and power led him to see an enemy where a lesser man would have never thought to look.

"That, my beloved people, is my story. The things I have spoken are true. Big Turtle knows this and can speak for me."

As Fighting Bear sat down, Big Turtle rose slowly to his feet. For several moments he looked solemnly around. "Our brother speaks the truth," he said. "It was in the spring that he came to me and told me of his plan. He laid it all out to me as he has told it here. He said that he would go through with it at some future time, though he did not say just when."

Big Turtle paused again to look about at his people. "In your faces I see the question you are asking: Has our brother been too harsh? Did Redbird have to suffer so terribly, and her mother and father too, as they sat at her bedside? Let me answer by asking you another question: Could it have been otherwise and the purpose still served? If our brother Fighting Bear were to leave us this very day for the Darkening Land, the Deer clan would be strong enough to stand without him. Their strength has come from what they endured together these last four days.

"You are asking if Redbird had to suffer so much. I say, ask yourselves another question: How many times have we seen it happen that one among us is stricken with illness or someone is filled with blueness and misery, and he turns his face to the Darkening Land without a fight—he chooses a happy reunion with his grandmothers over the pain and suffering of staying on this side. How many times have we seen two people afflicted by the same illness and one fights to stay with us while the other runs to his grandmothers. Our daughter Redbird has learned to suffer. She has learned how to fight to stay with us. She no longer needs her uncle's power to coax her back from the trail to the Darkening Land.

"We are not looking for our brother Fighting Bear to leave us. We hope that he will yet be with us for many years. But no one knows when his time will come. Today Redbird and Soaring Hawk are no longer children. Today these two can stand alone in the world. The ordeal was very hard for them. It brought anguish to Easy Dancer and Black Fox. It brought sorrow to those of us who were watching with them. But in his heart Fighting Bear felt that this had to be. In my heart I agree with him. I know that in your hearts you also will agree, for none of us would want to see the day when there would be no more Deer people in our town. The Deer people are the weakest among us in numbers. Their hearts must be the strongest."

As Big Turtle stepped back, the people sat in silence. "I have spoken," he said. He turned to Fighting Bear, who was sitting apart from the others, and he offered his hand to help him to his feet. The people also rose, and they began to talk quietly among themselves. Then Fighting Bear moved among them, and one by one they greeted him, offering their support and expressing their compassion.

Soaring Hawk stood apart and watched. The weight of all that had happened seemed to press upon him unbearably. He could not think anymore. He could not even move. He wished for the people to leave. He wanted a bed to lie on, a place to be alone. He wanted to sleep. Surely everything would seem better after he had slept. But first he had to see Redbird. He began making his way to the bed where she sat. She watched him come, her eyes shining with tears. He stopped beside her and tried to speak, but though his heart was full, no words would come.

She said to him, "You look so tired, Brother. You must eat now and sleep."

"You too, Sister." Tears sprang to his eyes, but he brushed them away. "I must go speak to Fighting Bear," he said. "I have to tell him that what he did was right."

"Yes, go tell him that. He should hear us say it. Tell him for me too. Tell him that everything is all right."

Soaring Hawk stood in the yard of his homestead taking in the excitement of the day. The town was overflowing with people who had come from hamlets and villages up and down the river for tomorrow's New Corn Festival. Some were staying in camps beyond the town, and others were crowding into the homesteads of friends and kinsmen. The Deer homestead was as teeming with people as the others, and in the midst of the commotion, old Owl sat beneath the shade of the big oak tree and told stories to a group of wide-eyed youngsters.

On the morning Owl had come down from the mountains with Soaring Hawk, he had stood on the outskirts of Raventown wondering whether or not to go home; it was at that moment he had decided to end his lonely exile. He moved back with his relatives, and now he came every day to the Deer homestead. There he sat for hours at a time unfolding to Soaring Hawk the power and mystery of his great vision.

Soaring Hawk would not have minded sitting with Owl today and listening to some of the stories he was telling to the children, but he had something much more important to do. He was waiting now for it to be time to go, and he paced in the yard, a little excited, a little nervous. People kept coming up and talking to him, congratulating him on being elected to sit in the festival danceground with the men this year. He smiled and mumbled polite words, but his mind was on other things. The sun was creeping much too slowly across the sky.

At last he walked out of the yard and began making his way along the crowded path. Before he had gone very far, he saw a strange procession coming toward him through the throng of people. In the lead was Scratcher, and trailing behind him in single file were all three of his wives. Each wife carried a large pot that Soaring Hawk knew was filled with food, and Scratcher himself was bearing a whole hind quarter of a deer. This was the second time since Redbird's ordeal that Scratcher had come bringing gifts to the Deer people.

Scratcher, it seemed, had had quite a scare. He actually *had* gone on a hunting trip early on the day that Redbird had fallen so terribly ill, but his prey had been four-footed deer, not the two-footed kind. Returning home the next day, he had been met at the edge of the woods by a nephew who informed him of what was happening and warned him of the suspicions in the town. Scratcher had seen at once the trouble he was in. Everyone knew how he had been acting toward Fighting Bear and the Deer people, and he would have had a hard time convincing them now that this thing with Redbird was not of his doing. And he knew that if Redbird died, the Deer people would not rest until they had avenged her death. With his own ill will Scratcher had laid a trap for himself, and all he could do was go back to the woods to hide. He stayed hidden throughout the ordeal, but in the end it had worked out all right for him. Now he was the perfect picture of good-will as he tried to make sure that such a thing did not happen to him again.

So it was that on seeing Soaring Hawk in the path, Scratcher stopped to greet him.

"It's always good to see you, Son," said Scratcher, and it sounded to Soaring Hawk as if he really meant it. "You should come visit us at our homestead sometime. In fact, why don't you come tonight? Some of my wives' people will be there—Chestnut Bread, I think, and some others." The Paint women exchanged knowing smiles, and Soaring Hawk felt embarrassed, though pleased nonetheless with the invitation.

"Thank you for asking me," he said, nodding to the wives. "I would enjoy making a visit to your homestead. And you, of course, are always welcome in ours."

"We are on our way there right now," said Scratcher, hoisting the meat on his shoulder again.

"They will be glad to see you." Soaring Hawk smiled, and bidding them farewell, he started on his way again.

All the way to the river the path was crowded with people going and coming with water jars. But once he waded across and started up the trail on the other side, the excitement of the festival began to fade away behind him. Soaring Hawk was filled with an excitement of his own, and as he moved along the trail, his anticipation grew with every step until at last he came to the red oak that leaned across the water. Then his heart fell like a bird shot from the sky. No one was there. Crushed with disappointment, he turned to go back.

Just then there was movement in the bushes and Chestnut Bread stepped out onto the path. Soaring Hawk turned to her with a smile. "I thought you had forgotten," he said.

"I wouldn't forget."

"It took me longer to get here than I thought it would. Have you ever seen so many people?"

"I never have," said Chestnut Bread. "Some of them have even been coming up this path. I had to hide to keep from being seen."

"Come on, then. I know where we can go." He took her by the hand and led her back through the woods, leaving the trail far behind. They came at last to a little clearing, a lovely spot with a grassy floor and a blue circle of sky overhead. A tiny stream ran by one side, and they could hear the gentle murmur of its song.

"It's beautiful," said Chestnut Bread. "I've never been here before."

"I don't know if anyone ever comes here but me. Once I almost showed it to June Bug and Hard Mush, but then I changed my mind. I'm glad now that I did."

Chestnut Bread sat down in the grass near the stream. "What do those two think of you sitting with the men this year?"

"Oh, they act all right about it—maybe they're just a little jealous. I would be too, I suppose. They tease me a lot by saying it was all a hoax. They say Fighting Bear and I got together and decided that if I beat Fighting Bear at something, the council would vote to let me sit with the men. They say Redbird helped out by pretending to be so sick."

"They shouldn't joke about that," said Chestnut Bread. "They wouldn't if they had seen her lying there. It was frightening."

Soaring Hawk sat down beside her. "She told me how you helped her hang on," he said. "She said you were the one who kept her from turning her face to the west. She said our grandmother was calling her from the Darkening Land, but that you kept calling her from this side, and it was you she made herself listen to. And Fighting Bear told me how you ran out to him when you heard the raven-mocker and helped him get back in the house in time."

Chestnut Bread looked at the ground. "I did what I

could," she said softly. She was quiet for a moment, and then she said, "Did she tell you how it was when the sickness had hold of her?"

"Not very much. Only about how you helped. There are a lot of things she doesn't tell me. Things she would tell a sister."

"I'm glad you're not her sister," Chestnut Bread murmured with a smile.

Soaring Hawk's heart was flying again. He moved closer to her. Without looking at him she reached out her hand. He took it and held it for a moment. Then he lay back in the grass and rested his head in her lap. She stroked his hair gently, and he closed his eyes in happiness.

"She told me how it was with her," Chestnut Bread said softly. "Through the whole thing she was very worried about whether she would be able to carry on the lineage. She said she was plagued with dreams in which either she was barren and could have no children or else she was having one child after another and all were boys. She said that even when she was awake those same thoughts were with her and that at times she wanted to die just to get away from them. But after you cured her, all that went away, and now she dreams of pleasant things. She tells me that she dreams every night that her homestead is running over with daughters and that you have to keep coming home to build more houses for her."

"Where do I keep coming home from?"

"From your wife, of course."

Soaring Hawk opened his eyes in time to catch the smile on her face. He looked away from her, up into the clear blue sky. He listened and in the stillness he could hear Long Man's song rising softly from the waters of the tiny stream.

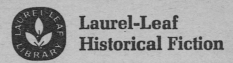

Laurel-Leaf
Historical Fiction

☐ ## CEREMONY OF INNOCENCE
by James Forman $1.25 (91177-X)

Hans and Sophie were students at Munich University in 1942. Although neither wanted to be a martyr, the scourge of Nazism was at its height and the burden of conscience forced them to act. With the Gestapo on their trail, they courted death daily. "Superb, sensitive, honest and compelling."—*The New York Times Book Review*

☐ ## FAWN
by Robert Newton Peck 95¢ (92488-X)

Fawn, a boy of the wilderness whose father was a French colonist and whose grandfather was a Mohawk warrior, is caught up in the turmoil of the French and Indian Wars. "Sensitively written narrative full of wilderness flavor."
—*The Booklist*

☐ ## TRANSPORT 7-41-R
by T. Degens $1.25 (99003-3)

Set in a cattle car filled with German refugees in April of 1946, this narrative of death and compassion traces the voyage of human freight from a Russian-occupied sector to the bombed-out city of Cologne. A thirteen-year-old girl protects an old man and a dead woman during the treacherous journey toward an uncertain future. "Stark and vigorous, this has the quality and authenticity of a documentary film."—*Book World*

REMEMBER IT DOESN'T GROW ON TREES

ENERGY CONSERVATION -
IT'S YOUR CHANCE TO SAVE, AMERICA
Department of Energy, Washington, D.C.

DATE DUE

5/6/81			
NOV 24 '81			
DEC 8 '81			
OCT 16 '95			